Dewar, Evelyn

Perfumes of Arabia.

PERFUMES OF ARABIA

Perfumes of Arabia

EVELYN DEWAR

Walker and Company
New York

All the characters and events portrayed in this story are fictitious.

First published in the United States of America in 1974 by the Walker Publishing Company, Inc.

Published simultaneously in Canada by Fitzhenry & Whiteside, Limited, Toronto.

ISBN: 0-8027-5302-7.

Library of Congress Catalog Card Number: 73-93935.

Printed in the United States of America.

10 9 8 7 6 5 4 3 2 1

For Christopher
with love

Chapter One

ROBERT'S WIFE HAD SWORN to kill Duncan Stuart. She had a cheap Smith and Wesson revolver which she had got through mail order when Robert was teaching in the United States. There had been some ammunition for it, too, but she was terribly nervous of having firearms in the house in case one of the children got hold of them or there was an accident, so she had long ago left the cartridges somewhere. She said she had learned to shoot in America too, at some class for housewives run by the local police, but I don't really believe she had ever fired that thing or that she could ever have got an aim on Duncan and squeezed the trigger. That's why I never did anything about the gun, of course. I mean, what point in telling the police she had a gun she'd smuggled into England and had no licence for? She kept it locked up, never played with it or got it out to look at it or made a drama of it. And yet she gained from it a therapeutic calm through the bad years. It made her quietly sure that one day she would kill the man she hated.

I was very fond of Joanna. At that time I could close my eyes and see her in my mind. When I was in England I used to go and spend weekends with them at their house near Guildford where Robert was teaching at the University. Every time I longed to see her. Not because she was beautiful but because she was peculiar. She had long red hair which hung down her back and got in the way when she hugged the children. Her face was white and she used to wear a lot of black stuff round her eyes which made her look rather tragic. It was a habit she had picked up in El Aasima where the eyes of the Arab women are dark with kohl. When I see them I am reminded of Joanna, but when I see Joanna I am reminded of no one but herself, the food she cooks, the children she frolics with, the husband, my friend, with whom she is in love.

I thought about this as I drove down from London on the Saturday afternoon. It had rained the night before and the thick trees beside the road smelled warm and summery, a delicious smell when one has been starved of England as I had been. Working in the desert I had been starved of woodland and starved of my friends. Now I was restored to both with eight weeks of home leave from Arabia stretching ahead of me like an eternity of happiness. Robert had wasted no time in inviting me down. Now he came forward to greet me as I arrived. He ran across the gravel to close the white gates behind me, to knock aside the cow parsley and nettles on the verge, to let me out of my hired car into the arms of his waiting family.

When I tried to thank him he would have none of it.

'My home is your home,' he said and it was true. Even when they had had nowhere to live it had been true, and I had been homeless as well. His two children, my god-children, hung back with their mother, not remembering over my twelve months' absence that they had ever known me before, but Joanna pushed them forward with murmured, happy words. She took their hands, she ran her fingers across their shining heads, she bent to whisper and then straightened up, radiant, to meet me and take my tanned arm in her white one and kiss me on the cheek.

That evening when the children were asleep we had a long slow dinner. We ate melon with prawns, then a rough, subtle Corsican daube redolent of the Mediterranean I had just left behind, and ended with a child's treat of strawberries and cream. They had grown the strawberries themselves and there was masses of fruit that year. Some were small like wild wood strawberries, some large and glossy; all were delicious. Joanna laughed when I praised them; she seemed to have grown them by accident. She seemed so careless of her good fortune in having Robert and that home, that little isolated Paradise in which to live.

'To your happiness.' I drank to both of them. 'May I always be able to share it.'

She put her warm hand in my hand for an instant. 'You shared our unhappiness, didn't you?' she said.

Looking at her young face, it was difficult for me to remember that she had ever been unhappy.

'That's so long ago,' I said.

'Four and a half years.'

Robert's hair had gone white above the ears in that time, but otherwise he seemed recovered. He was pouring out the duty-free brandy I had brought them and he seemed relaxed, at ease with himself. His hands did not tighten on the bottle at any memory of his disgrace. I thought him admirably able to live with it. Indeed several trinkets from the suq at El Aasima, a rough wooden camel, a leather pouf, still bore witness to his previous existence with Super Oil. He had even hung on to one of those inflatable globes which the company had handed out one Christmas with their emblem brashly printed on the base. I'd had one in my office once, then lost it somewhere. But I was still in the company; I could always get another. For Robert it was different; they had kicked him out, or rather Duncan had. Afterwards I had had the unenviable task of meeting them off the El Aasima plane, Joanna distraught, homeless, pregnant, with David, her eldest child, clutched to her, and Robert, furious and yet somehow cowed by his summary dismissal.

Maybe I had always liked Robert for the very qualities Duncan had mistrusted in him. Robert was a stolid, righteous man who probed and questioned almost all the precepts of the company. He had a fiendish vigour for finding out and a talent for compulsive improvements which, though often impertinent, had the merit of sending profits up. People called him a whizz-kid. Certainly he was an enthusiast and the years when he was second in charge at El Aasima were really the golden years. But the ideas that Robert put forward were never quite in character with Super Oil International. Duncan, who had to deal with them, sensed that. Robert was something of a thorn in his flesh.

Duncan's moment came in the middle of the summer when the two of them had a final explosive quarrel about when they should take their respective leave. Duncan had booked a holiday in Scotland. Robert hadn't prepared for anything. He had been sweating it out for two years without home leave but he had always felt he could not be spared. At last, with the worst of the summer on him and with Joanna pregnant and exhausted, longing for the sea and the cool, he demanded an immediate holiday. Tempers fray in that climate. Duncan took the opportunity to throw the rule book at Robert and point out that he was claiming as a right what was only a privilege. I do not know what they said to each other but it ended with Robert leaving the company.

For Robert it was a bolt from the blue. His request for a holiday had been so trivial. However, it wasn't the request which Duncan held against him, it was the tone of the request betraying so well Robert's undesirable attitude. There was no particular reparation Robert could make for this. He resigned under pressure. He packed his things and left.

He had to leave a lot behind. He and Joanna had expected to stay out in El Aasima or similar places for years and so they had saved nothing. Everything he earned they had spent on their house and garden. There was a paddling pool for the baby, ice buckets and extra fans to stir the unbearable summer air, fine light clothes for tropic nights, a Land-Rover for hunting trips in the desert and a mass of paraphernalia which would be of no more use to them in London than a simple bedou tent.

When they came back we went to Marks and Spencer and

bought warmer clothes for the family. Luckily Robert got an unimportant job at an American university and they began again from scratch in a tiny, stuffy apartment neither of them could bear. I tried to persuade Robert that he ought to be back in oil or dealing with the Arabs in some way, but he simply would not listen. He was disenchanted with the Arab world and unattracted by the great oil companies which had once had his undivided loyalty. He was loyal now to no one but himself, and Joanna, as ever, was loyal to no one but to him. She was eaten by bitterness, bitter enough to kill.

My darling Joanna who was so gay and generous bore no trace that night of what she had had to bear all those years before. She leaned back in a big armchair with her hands relaxed in her lap and her head on one side as she listened to my news. I had tact enough not to mention Duncan and she came and went with coffee and fresh drinks until the evening grew slow and sleepy and it was time for all of us to go to bed.

The next day we spent playing with the children. The sand was beginning to wash away from my mind. Judy and David squealed and splashed in their blue paddling pool; we lazed on rugs in the shade and read substantial sheets of Sunday paper, bestirring ourselves only to pick yet more strawberries for supper. It was a glorious day and I did not want to leave, but I had things to attend to in London the following week and I had no choice.

As she took me out to the car Joanna took my arm and came close beside me.

'Mark, I still hate Duncan,' she confided in me.

'I know, I know, Joanna,' I tried to comfort her. 'You have good reason, God knows.'

She smiled. I think I had reassured her, because she went back to her husband with a smile and together they stood waving at the gate as I swung the car round and away between the sweetly smelling trees.

The next Wednesday I read that Duncan was dead. His name was in the Deaths column on the back page of *The Times* and it forced me to get out of bed, root around for my slippers and look for my old copies of the paper in case there was a proper account of the accident. There was indeed and I was cross with myself for having missed that paragraph before. Duncan, his wife and their two student sons had been killed when their car collided with a lorry on the road linking El Aasima with its airport fifteen miles away. 'British Oil Man Killed', said the headline. I shaved, washed, dressed and rang the London office. I didn't feel anything. I couldn't really be glad about such a ghastly business but I honestly couldn't bring myself to be sorry.

'I've just heard about Duncan,' I said when I was put through to Michaelson's office. 'I'm so sorry.'

'Yes, it's a frightful business. I was hoping you'd get in touch.'

'I thought you might be.'

Life was like that when one hadn't a wife or children. One was sent off at short notice to plug any gap that came up. There was no one to take with me and no one to miss me if I went alone. Duncan had been negotiating fresh agreements from time to time and would eventually have to be replaced at the highest level. Meanwhile I was sent out as a stop-gap to tie up any loose ends and get his things packed up.

'O.K. Of course I'll go,' I said, and when I had put the receiver down I began to swear at the whole bloody organisation which had mucked up my leave.

I spent the rest of the day in the office mugging up the files. That spread into the next morning. Then I rang up Joanna and said I would be coming down to collect my casual clothes which I'd left there with every expectation of wearing them again over the holiday.

'Duncan's dead, you know,' I said gently.

'Yes. Robert said.'

'You'll be able to get rid of that gun now anyway.' It was a feeble sort of joke. From the other end of the line she said,

'Oh, I don't know. One of his side might try and get me next. It's a battle, isn't it? It goes on.'

'His sons were killed too, Joanna.'

She caught her breath. 'Oh, that's dreadful, Mark.'

'Both of them. His wife too.'

'I don't care about her.'

I don't believe she did and I had no good reason for holding it against her. Certainly Duncan's wife wouldn't have cared a fig for Joanna.

I drove down in rather more of a hurry than usual. It was a greyish morning and when I got there Joanna was out in the garden hanging out the washing. Her arms were lifted above her head as she reached for the row of blowing white nappies. Colours floated on the wind: jerseys crucified upon the line. When she had finished she picked up the big, wickerwork basket and came round the corner of the house. The children were with her but this time they recognised me and came forward to hold my hands.

'I didn't have time to sew your button on,' she said, but she had packed my case which was standing in the hall. The children began to play ball round our legs. In the confined space their noise was fantastic. Joanna was laughing. I wanted to take her in my arms and kiss her.

'You mustn't,' she said, laughing and shaking her head. 'Mark, you ought to get married again. You ought to look for someone to marry.'

Going out to the car again she suddenly smiled.

'What is it?' I asked, thinking that she was amused at the idea of me with a new bride. She shrugged. 'The honeysuckle,' she pointed out. The house was covered in honeysuckle up to the front bedroom windows. 'Duncan will never have flowers again.' All her little pleasures must have been magnified that day, now that Duncan could not share them.

'Forgive him now,' I said. 'Let it rest. He's dead. Forgive him.'

'There's no longer anyone left to forgive.'

I wound down the driver's window and she leaned close to the car.

'If you go to our old house in El Aasima, give it my love.'

I bent and kissed her hand as it rested on the window frame. 'O.K. I'll do that. Take care of yourself.'

Chapter Two

I GOT THE NIGHT plane. When one has flown as much as I have, one no longer expects too much of the air hostess's eyes as she offers one a drink. I took cognac that flight and drank it all the way. Journeys end in lovers' meeting, they say, but I had never found the woman I would have liked to be my second wife, with whom I could have envisaged another forty years or so of happiness. I was alone and not in love. I wondered about Duncan because, although many seemed to hate him, he had at least been loved, which was more than I could say for myself.

The company publish a sort of 'Who's Who' of their major personnel and I usually check it before leaving for anywhere new. Sometimes it holds clues which later on will help me to deal with my colleagues. When I looked up Duncan Stuart I was expecting to find problems. A long childless marriage, ten unrelieved years in the Arabian Gulf, unusually quick promotion, any of these stresses could have helped to explain Duncan. Yet Duncan's entry in the book told me nothing. He had been of a different generation, seventeen years older than I. He had married at twenty-eight, the right age for a good company man to acquire a wife. His two sons had been born early in the marriage; there was no problem there. The boys had done well at school and had gone on to university. Duncan and his wife had been meeting the plane which brought them out for the long vacation. A happy family, one assumed.

On the career side Duncan was something of an oddity.

He had risen quickly but there was nothing to suggest why. He had been one of the legion of good public-school administrators swallowed up by British industry every year. Was Duncan hated because he was envied or had his comparative youth and lack of confidence made him too heavy handed with us who were under him? He had been newly promoted when he got rid of Robert and new brooms sweep clean.

I'd met him twice and what could I say about him? He was ambitious. He believed in the company and only the company. His speech was peppered with references to 'well-knit teams' and 'happy ships'. Management consultants scared him because he did not believe that outsiders could really understand Super Oil in the way that we insiders did. He called us a 'happy family' yet whatever his metaphor, a team, a ship, a family, it was clear to us that we were the crew and he was always the captain. This was not what he intended, of course, but he was a man who had been born and bred to hierarchies, and he could not shake off the habit.

I wondered how his boys had reacted to it. I wondered how Duncan had seen the modern world and whether he had been disappointed in what his power had brought him. Was he constantly having to bolster his faith in the old order by sweeping aside young men like Robert who might have set doubts nagging?

I fixed my company badge in my lapel so that I would be recognised for what I was and pushed my way through Customs as quickly as Arab courtesies permitted. The Battys, the young couple who met me at the barrier, had been to a party. They had friends with them who were laughing and talking. The bright summer dresses shocked me somehow. It didn't seem right that they had spent the night hours drinking and dancing while Duncan was dead.

I'd tried to prepare myself for the solemnity which always follows the death of a man. I wanted to be quiet, to be shown to his house and go quietly through his things, to find my feet in an unobtrusive way. I had been drinking on the plane but that was more of a soporific. The young people made me feel old and disapproving and I could not bring myself to spend any time with them in the bar. I wanted to go straight up to bed and prepare myself for the grisly task ahead of me.

It was a modern hotel. My room was cool and white with an air conditioner in full blast and plastic flowers in a green vase on the dressing table. Even though it was four o'clock in the morning, a silent, white-robed servant brought me iced water in a thermos. Apart from the air conditioner it was very quiet. I could no longer hear the crickets in the trees. I got my pyjamas out of my hold-all and opened my suitcase; Joanna had folded everything very neatly. She had mended my shirt after all. I lifted it out and found a strange shape in the corner of the case: I pulled at the tissue paper and out fell a small toy bear, very brown and worn. A mascot from Joanna with a folded note of paper.

Dear Mark,

Judy insists on your having Bear for company. Please bring him back as I think he will be missed terribly this end.

J.

Judy had written her name too in big letters.

I propped the note up by my mirror and put the bear by the bed. I fell asleep very quickly but I was thinking all the time of how nice it would have been in England.

I spent the next morning drinking Arab coffee with Sayed Mohammed Ismael, an Under Secretary at the Ministry of Petroleum Affairs. We talked in a leisurely way of many things, of my time out in the caravans with the early surveys, of his sons and his rose garden, of the plans for the new university extension to house a Department of Petroleum Studies. Although we began by commiserating with each other over Duncan's death, we did not mention him again, nor did we discuss the oil concessions which he had renegotiated for Super Oil under the previous government. It was almost one o'clock when I left the government offices and walked down to the row of yellow taxis waiting under the palm trees which fringed the public square.

Duncan's house was a low, white bungalow. It was not old but the fierce sun and desert wind weather new buildings very quickly. The house looked old. It stood in its own garden which after a week of neglect was dying for lack of water. The rose beds had opened into yellow cracks and the lawn was scorched brown. Round the garden was a high wall with a gate which locked. I had a key and let myself in. The khamseen had left red dust on the paths and the verandas. My shoes slid in it as I climbed the steps to the front door. It was very hot and the sweat was running down behind my ears. I had expected it to be cooler indoors because our managers' houses have air conditioners and coolers in every room, but Duncan's house had been shut up with every window and shutter closed and no air moved from room to room. Some servant seemed to have kept the dust at bay indoors and the dead man's possessions remained untouched.

Many times since my arrival I had said how sorry I was that Duncan was dead. It was an automatic form of words. I never really felt sorry at all until I stepped into his living room and saw his photographs hanging round the walls. He was obsessed by photography and these brilliant black and white prints, beautifully framed and mounted, were things he had made; here at last was his imagination at work, his vision of the Arab towns he had lived in, the ruins he had visited, the Gulf coast with its little sailing ships, their triangular sails spread in the streaks and shadows of a tropical sunset. There was a portrait of Mrs Stuart with her untidy hair falling round her face. I felt sick with the heat and with hunger and with the knowledge that I too would die. I was sick with fear. Then someone sprang at me from behind, pulled my arms behind my back and I was pressed against the sweaty folds of an old jallabiyah.

The man who held me trapped was younger than I, and smaller, but he was stronger and his wild appearance frightened me. His jallabiyah was caught up in a belt in which was stuck an unsheathed knife, and his turban was piled on top of his head like that of a young warrior. He was dark skinned, lithe, with handsome flashing eyes and teeth, and his Arabic was strange to me for it was that of the hills where I had never been. He did not seem inclined to talk and though I protested at being held, he proceeded to open my jacket and pull out my wallet and papers from the inside pocket. Still keeping me under observation he withdrew to the table and began to go through my things. I expected that he would make off with my money and leave me to get back to the Battys' house, where I was supposed to be lunching, as best I could. He would probably take one or two things from the house as well, the radio, for instance, which he could sell in the suq without causing too much surprise. I lay back in the armchair into which he had pushed me and waited until he was satisfied.

Painstakingly he counted out my notes, my travellers' cheques and the five English pounds in my wallet. He looked at my passport, holding it upside down and starting from the back as Arabs tend to. He looked at the visiting card I had received from my host that morning in the Ministry of Petroleum, and I gathered from this exhibition of curiosity that the young man could not read. Finally he sorted out my few snapshots. There was one of my parents, one of Joanna and Robert with their children in the garden, one of a friend who had died. I didn't want to lose them and I tensed up when he touched them with his grubby fingers. It seemed an age before he pushed everything back into the wallet and brought it over to me.

I had been so intent on my photographs that I did not realise for a moment that he was offering me back my money as well. If he hadn't I am not sure what I would have done next. The sudden heat of El Aasima, into which I had been thrust the night before like bread into an oven, hardly fitted me for heroics. I was dripping with sweat. All I wanted was a cold beer and my lunch. I wanted to get out of that house where other people seemed to be in control. Normally I am the one I like to be in control and I did not think I could handle the farouche creature who was now babbling at me in his unintelligible dialect. A few words I caught. A few salaams. He said he was the gaffir (the guard), he said he did not know me, or had not known me. He took me by the arm and showed me to the door and so I left. I hadn't much choice.

Nothing particularly alarming happened for the rest of that day. I had a calm lunch with Batty and his wife Pauline. Batty was in Robert's old job and I thought him very deferential, very eager to oblige. Just as he ought to be. He couldn't really be very pleased to see me. At the back of his mind perhaps he had had a greedy idea that with Duncan dead he would be in charge. But in rational moments he must have known he wouldn't be promoted that quickly. London would send a replacement for Duncan only too soon. And in the meantime there was myself. He talked to me over lunch about the things Duncan had had in mind. It was Duncan this and Duncan that and we discussed the business of going through his things and I told him about the gaffir jumping me and we laughed. Before I left and went back to the hotel the Battys invited me to a party that night way out in the new section of the town where the houses are like iced cakes and the gardens haven't had time to grow green.

A party is a party out there. They happen all the time because there is nothing else to do. It meant no disrespect for the dead. I had been wrong to think it did. The dead anyway are dead and buried in that heat inside twenty-four hours. So there was this party out on the floodlit lawn of a big white house belonging to BOAC. There was Beatles music on the record player and a lot of people I didn't know were circulating with frosty glasses of whisky and soda or gin and tonic. I met a hell of a lot of people who all said what a tragedy it was about Duncan and how much they would miss him, which I found vaguely embarrassing considering how I had resented him while he was alive. Eventually, to get away from the crowd, I thought I'd find myself a girl. There was one on the veranda with bright red hair like Joanna's but with it cropped short and in a slim white dress just right for the heat. I had seen her around in the office. I like girls with red hair and white dresses.

She looked up at me as I climbed the steps. 'Hallo,' she said. 'Have you found any clues yet?'

'I think you've got the wrong man,' I said, because though I liked boyish girls with red hair, I didn't like them mixing me up with other people.

'Oh I know who you are,' she said. 'You were in the office this evening. You're the man sent by London to find out who killed Duncan Stuart.'

'Just a moment,' I interrupted. 'Who says anybody killed him?'

'Oh, everyone,' she said. She shrugged at me. Those thin white shoulders. A white-robed waiter pushed past her with a tray of glasses.

'No one's told me.'

'Have you talked to anyone?'

'I've talked to Peter Batty and . . . '

'You've talked to the managers,' she said and dismissed them all. 'They don't know anything. They don't want to know.'

'So who says it wasn't an accident? Who? The Arabs?'

'Perhaps . . . but Europeans too. Everyone—except the managers obviously.' She gave me a pitying look.

'Why obviously?' I demanded.

'Otherwise they would have told you, wouldn't they?'

I didn't know about that. I was beginning not to know about quite a number of things.

'And you?' I asked in what I hoped was a bantering tone. 'Are you going to tell me?'

'Tell you what, Mr Patterson?' I glanced across the lawn to where her friends were talking beneath a scarlet outburst of bougainvillea. Her clear young voice seemed to carry to every corner of that dark garden.

'Anything you like,' I suggested. Her fingers were close to mine on the balustrade. I had meant to move mine closer. When I approach a girl at a party in a garden, I want the company of a pretty girl at a party; that's all. What I had got from the transparently innocent, freckled face was much nastier.

'All I can tell you,' she said, 'is that he'd driven to the airport and back dozens of times before and never come to grief.'

Chapter Three

THE ROAD TO THE airport is long and straight. In the rainy season they dig drainage ditches down either side and I suppose that if one is in too much of a hurry one can turn a car over in them. But this wasn't the rainy season. I got up very early next morning and drove that way: first through the residential development area where small groups of desert tribesmen who had drifted into town to become illiterate gangs of building workers were already starting the day's stint of labouring. The houses they were building were to be the city's best, preposterous crenellated villas sailing like white many-decked ships out of the edge of the desert. Then there was desert proper with the tarmac strip of road laid across it like a ribbon. The airport was just desert too, a tarmac landing strip in the scrub about fifteen miles out from the town. It was an inoffensive strip of road but it was the farthest anyone ever went from the town in an ordinary saloon car. Further out on desert tracks people usually took a Land-Rover.

When I'd done that bit of homework I turned up at the office, knocked on Peter Batty's door and told him I was going to need a bit of secretarial help with the inventory.

'I suppose that means you want Carole,' he said bitterly.

'If Carole is the red-head I was talking to last night,' I said, 'you're absolutely right.'

Since Duncan was dead, Batty had inherited Carole as

his personal secretary and in our business that's a privilege you cling to.

'I'm going to do the inventory,' I said, 'and if I get jumped by your bloody guard today, Batty, I'll . . . '

'Funny him jumping you like that,' said Batty and he laughed.

'It wasn't a bit funny,' I retorted. 'By the way, who is he?'

'Best guard we've got. He sometimes worked as a suffragi for Duncan. Surprising that, because we had always thought he was a fanatical sectarian and would refuse to handle alcohol. But Mrs Stuart liked to have him around. With all the burglaries and break-ins you get here nowadays the women like to have a guard. Gives them a sense of security.'

'She felt insecure, did she?'

'Nervy woman, that. She didn't like her darling boys going off to England by air. Always afraid of bombs and terrorists and God knows what. Anyway Ali is our best gaffir. Our only real guard you might say, because all the others have been with us for donkey's years. They're so old they creak when they move. This lad lies in wait with a dagger. Spear, sword, stick, give him anything you like. He's a professional. He prides himself on it.'

'Lucky to have him.'

'That's what we think.'

'Do you have a guard on your house, Batty?'

'No,' he said calmly, 'I don't believe in it.'

'Batty,' I said casually, because he was relaxed and it seemed the right moment. 'There is apparently a rumour going the rounds that your late lamented boss was done in by someone who resented being bossed; what do you think about that?'

'London rumour?' he asked.

'Sorry, no. Local rumour. I suppose you got all the details of the accident from the police?'

'God, yes. All the nauseating details. I haven't published them.'

'Can I see?'

'They're all yours. Go ahead.'

'You tell me about it first.'

'He drove fast. Had a Jaguar XJ6 he was very proud of. He was overtaking a suq lorry and there was something coming in the other direction.'

'What?'

'A taxi.'

'Was the taxi driver killed too?'

'Yes.'

'Any passengers?'

'It was empty. Going out to the airport to collect a fare.'

'Any witnesses?'

'The lorry driver.'

I opened the file. There was a map of that bit of the road with the position of the vehicles plotted onto it.

'Did you identify the bodies?'

'It was burned out. I identified the vehicle.'

He sat in silence chewing his fingernail and I didn't know what to say.

It was exactly as he had said. It was all there in the file: the police report and the lorry driver's evidence. I shut the file and put it down on his desk. In that air-conditioned office high over the town one was in an ivory tower. I knew what it was like in the trailers by the oil rigs. A different world.

'Any repercussions?' I asked him. 'Any trouble from the locals?'

He shook his head. 'No. Of course the taxi driver's family could simply be biding their time. They may be onto us yet for compensation.'

'I doubt it,' I said, 'it's over a week now.'

'I doubt it too and yet, and yet . . . ' he got up. 'Why,' he asked me with sudden genuine intensity, 'why did they take so much trouble to prove it was Duncan's driving that caused the accident, if they didn't hope that we would be forced to provide for the dependants of the other man who was killed?'

'You think it's a fabrication, then? You think it was the taxi which was overtaking and was on the wrong side of the road'?

'That makes better sense than Duncan doing a damnfool thing like that in his car.'

'But you could tell from the damage to the car, surely.'

'I couldn't tell,' he said.

'Then you think that this rumour about his having been murdered just might be relevant?'

'No, that's nonsense. It's just that the details of the accident are anyone's guess. However, it doesn't make much difference since they're dead now, poor things. A dreadful business, dreadful.' Then his curiosity got the better of him. 'Who thinks Duncan was murdered?' he asked me.

I didn't tell him. I just made a mental note that that was one of the things I was going to have to discover.

Looking at the educated, naive and very English face of the young man behind the desk, I wondered why he hadn't found out. After all, he had been in charge of the shop for some time now. All Duncan's little kingdom had been Batty's to direct or investigate if he felt so inclined. But he hadn't. He had done nothing. I wondered what had happened while Duncan was on leave each year. Nothing, I supposed. Batty had done nothing and done it very well. Life is like that in the Arab world. Everything can wait until another day. Bukra, bukra, tomorrow, there is always tomorrow.

This time, though, things were different. There was a new oil lease to be competed for and a labour agreement to work out with the embryo union our men had been prompted to set up. Duncan had been doing all that: Duncan and London between them but mostly Duncan because Duncan knew the Arabs here and knew their way of doing things. I knew them too but there was a big difference between Duncan and me. Beneath his austerity, beneath the formality with which he approached them, there lay Duncan's insatiable passion for all things Arabic. A whole generation of Englishmen who learned Arabic and went out to the Middle East succumbed as he did to the romance of the desert and its people. Where else could Duncan have been so liberated from his provincial Scottish background? On Burns' night he put on his kilt and danced reels with the rest of the expatriates and pretended that he longed to go home. But he didn't really. His true feelings were revealed in his photographs hung on the walls of his house—vistas of sand dunes, a bedou face weathered by desert winds, intricate prayer mats and souvenirs of his travels. Duncan had loved the Arabs and I hoped very much that they hadn't taken it into their heads to kill him. There would have been no justice in that. But Carole said Duncan had been murdered and Carole was a reliable girl.

She came in at that moment, summoned by her boss, and as she pushed open the door she gave me a straight piercing look trying to fathom perhaps whose side I was on.

I wasn't on her side at that moment. 'Come on, girl,' I said, 'have you got the papers?'

She held out a thin file. It held only one sheet of paper: a list of the furniture that was in Duncan's villa.

'It's already been checked,' said Batty helpfully. 'Everything's there.'

'I didn't come out here to check up on your chairs and tables,' I said with as much patience as I could muster. The company had sent me out on behalf of the Stuart family. I had to go through his personal possessions and see they got safely returned to his sister in Kensington. Items unlikely to be of use in London or which would fetch a good price locally, I intended to sell. What a job, raking over a dead man's things to see what they would fetch.

'Did you check this inventory yourself?' I asked Batty.

'Yes. I could have sent one of the lads down but I thought I'd do it myself.'

'I hope that when you came away you brought his photographic equipment with you and put it away in some safe place.'

'Photographic equipment?' he asked blankly.

'Cameras, lenses . . .'

'There were none. I saw none.'

I would have to go to the house myself, of course, but if he was right and there was no camera, then we had already been robbed, and all his precautions with arrogant young gaffirs were to no point. The house must have been left wide open to whoever wanted the pickings and it was his fault.

I saw he knew it. Gradually it sank in.

'Come on, Carole,' I said. 'Let's get going.'

The girl was nervous. In the car she kept clasping and unclasping her hands in her lap. I didn't know if it was me she was frightened of or going to the house. But she looked so miserable that I wondered why on earth I had brought her with me. I didn't really need her except for company and it didn't look as if she was going to be much good for that.

I had learned my lesson now. When we got out of the car at Duncan's gate I clapped my hands together and called for Ali. He came running up from the back veranda and I told him he could go off duty for an hour. He didn't go; he came with us into the house and I had to shout at him before he would leave us alone and I could set to work.

Duncan's personal papers were easy to get at. He had one of those metal boxes which Rymans sell for keeping household files in. It was locked and I had a key. It didn't look as if anyone else had been there before me. I opened the thing and pulled out the file tagged 'Insurance'. It was as I thought: there was some correspondence and a couple of household policies which gave a complete inventory of each item worth more than £50. It is curious how the most careful of men will leave this document lying around to guide any burglar who happens to come along.

That day I was the burglar. I went round the house picking up all the items on his list. There were two rings and a brooch belonging to his wife, an oil painting of a bridge, some hi-fi equipment and a nice clock, also one of those expensive short-wave radio sets you need for listening to the BBC overseas service when you live in the back of beyond. It was Japanese. I found everything except his cameras. Usually the radio set and the jewellery are the first things to go. It was odd how nothing was missing except the cameras. He could have had one with him in the car that final afternoon, possibly two if he had taken his movie camera along too, but Duncan had possessed four cameras and I didn't think he'd taken all four to the airport that day. He wasn't the sort of man to carry four cameras.

Carole and I carried all the stuff out to the car. It was quite heavy because we took along all the family silver for good measure, and his Persian rugs, too. We'd almost finished when Ali came back and lent us a hand with the rolls of carpet. It was about midday and very hot and I still had to question the girl. On the other hand I didn't like to park the car with all Duncan's valuables in it so we drove back to the office and got Batty to organise the unloading. While he was absorbed in this I shouted up a taxi from the rank opposite under the trees and took Carole off to the hotel. We needed a drink after our exertions. We sat on the terrace and I ordered lemonade and we ate a lot of fresh peanuts and pistachios and washed them down with the icy lemon. Life wasn't so bad.

The terrace was large and crowded. Almost all the tables were full and the waiters were busy taking orders. No one was the slightest bit interested in us.

'Carole,' I began, 'you said some not very nice things to me last night. Have you thought better of it this morning?'

'I suppose so.' She gave a little laugh. It was a half-hearted apology. Last night her suspicions had been genuine enough.

'Come on,' I encouraged her. 'You are the only person who has mentioned murder. I'm afraid that means you must tell me where and how the idea came to you.'

For I had come to the conclusion that she was not a person of many ideas. She was pretty and she was happy in a difficult place where not many English girls were truly happy. Carole had surmounted the sweat and fatigue. I liked to see her neat, clean dresses and the confident way in which she arranged her bare, well-showered legs as she sat on the public terrace. She was not a girl to make a fool of herself with fantasies. If the word 'murder' came from her it was specific and down to earth.

'Only me?' she asked, concerned. 'The idea didn't come to me in particular. I suppose it dawned on all of us.' She was moving the long spoon round and round in the lemon juice trying to dissolve the sugar which lay at the bottom of the glass.

'Who is "all of us"?' I asked.

'The girls. All the girls from the office. We had arranged a party that night and by the time we heard about the accident it was too late to cancel it. It was a curry party in Mick's flat and we had some of the marines in from the American Embassy. The girls were getting the food ready, all of us together, when Mick came back from the suq and said that Mr Batty had been called by the police and a lot of people were at the office and Mr and Mrs Stuart were dead. He didn't tell us any more. He didn't have any details, so we naturally thought they'd been killed.'

'Deliberately, you mean?'

'I suppose so. I didn't think about it very carefully.'

'But you all talked about it?'

'Yes.'

'In front of your servants?'

She saw at once that this annoyed me, for she said quickly, 'Mmm . . . but not seriously. We were just talking about it. I think some of us felt guilty because we hadn't taken the possibility seriously and now it had happened.'

At last she laid down the spoon and her swirling drink became still in the icy glass. She leaned back in her wicker chair and looked at me.

'But if it was an accident, then we don't have to worry. There was nothing we could have done.'

'Nothing,' I interrupted, 'but let's get this straight. You and some of the other girls, the English girls, from the office were expecting this to happen?'

'Not expecting, no. But when it happened it seemed predictable.'

'Why? What gave you all the idea?'

'It was Mrs Stuart. She often came into the office with letters for the post or to pick up her husband after work. She used to stop and chat with us and ask us how we were getting on and tell us how her sons were doing at university. She got to like us, I think. She liked us out of necessity. You know how it is overseas with so few new people to talk to and all of us so far from home. She was supposed to keep an eye on us, so she talked to us even though we bored her.'

I understood perfectly. It was the convention of such places. Indeed that was how I had first met Joanna. We were in the Gulf then. I had come in from the drilling camp to Bahrein because my mother was dying. There was no plane out that night so Robert took me back home with him to meet his wife and stay the night. I had not bored Joanna, nor they me, and after that I always had a place with them. We travellers pretend that we like to travel alone but when it comes to the point we need a family. We are all up for adoption.

Robert and Joanna had such a talent for making me feel at home that I like to think no one else would have been capable of it. But I know that if Joanna had not taken me in that night, someone else would have done, if only from duty, just as Mrs Stuart had forced herself to become acquainted with the office girls who did not interest her.

'It was nice of her to talk to you,' I said.

'Yes. We quite liked her until lately when she got desperate.'

'She thought someone was trying to kill her?'

'She was overwrought. We didn't take much notice. She often said things like they were going to "get" Mr Stuart and her and why didn't someone do something to stop it. Her eyes were red. She looked as if she cried a lot at home. We all thought she ought to have gone on leave.'

I couldn't make out why she had confided in the girls rather than in the police or even Peter Batty.

'Why did she tell you?' I asked. 'What could you do?'

'She said she couldn't tell Mr Batty or interfere with company policy. I think she thought we would understand because we were women. She didn't like to complain about what her husband was doing but she thought someone at least ought to know they were being victimised.'

'Did she say who was victimising her?'

'No. All she said to me was that she couldn't bear it any longer. She didn't say much to me. She talked a lot to Marjory. No one took any notice. It was all a bit sad.'

I too had seen wives begin to drink and lose track of reality but this didn't sound quite the same.

'So Mrs Stuart believed that she and her husband were going to be murdered?'

'Looking back, you know, I really think she did.'

'But no one else did?'

'No, no one at all. Just her and she told us. We thought she was crazy.'

'And she spoke mainly to Marjory?' I would have to speak to Marjory myself.

'Marjory was the eldest of us. She left about three months ago.'

Carole took out a handkerchief and wiped the sweat from her palms. She was quite right: it was far too hot to sit out at midday and after all that I felt she deserved some lunch. She refused my invitation because she said that her servant would have prepared something for her and she ought to go home and eat it. She asked me if I would like to go too. I would have liked it very much but at that moment it didn't seem judicious so I let her go.

I ordered some curling dry sandwiches for myself and sat at the table trying to sort things out in my own mind. One thing was clear. The fantastic rumour that the Stuarts had been murdered had not started in the Arab cafés or even in our office. It sprang from one embarrassing, almost neglected fact: the dead woman had been afraid, and afraid enough to confide in her husband's office girls, that she thought he was going to be murdered.

Chapter Four

THAT AFTERNOON I GOT down to work. I notified the police about the missing cameras. I applied for an export permit for Duncan's things, and signed a contract with a Greek packer for their shipment. I read up Duncan's papers about the proposed nationalisation of the banks and how this would affect us and drove round to look at two or three of our bungalows where the leases were coming up for renewal. All the time I thought about Duncan and the things Duncan had been interested in. He had been discussing whether we should move our offices into a new building. He had been struggling with plans for the new oil refinery down the coast and wondering whether the government would force us to build it. I thought about oil and forecasts and surveys and planning. I was concerned about the instability of the government and the chances of a revolution from the right and from the left.

Later I wandered round to the Ministry to see a friend there. Mohi el Din Saad had been to Cambridge on a British Council scholarship and was friends with almost all of us in the oil business. He was an Arab accustomed to moving among Europeans; he knew our ways and accepted them without in any way being seduced by them. He came to our parties and drank like a heathen but his father was a well-known lawyer and of a prominent family so at home Mohi el Din became a Moslem again. I spent hours in his company but never met his wife who remained in the purdah of her own household.

Mohi el Din had started out as a geologist and knew the desert well. I know the desert well, too, and it was like coming home to it to sit in his office sipping the bitter, cardamom-flavoured coffee. I forgot my irritation with Peter Batty and the trivial decisions he was incapable of making. (Had Duncan never allowed him to take any decisions for himself?) I forgot Carole's histrionic ideas and spent the evening with Mohi el Din and his brother. We sat in one of those walled Arab gardens which are so blissfully scented by their own jasmine bushes, gardens I associate with a soft drink made of apricots, with starry skies and the certainty of Arab friendship.

During that long, lovely evening I saw that I had been wrong to rush hither and thither setting the place to rights. I had ignored the tempo of the country itself and made myself conspicuous. I watched Mohi el Din pour the coffee from a clay pot that had worn a rich dark colour from the passage of time. Slowly, slowly one moves in that heat. It is not difficult in El Aasima to do nothing at all.

Over the next few days I began to let everyone see how little I was doing. I played tennis with the Battys at the club and I visited the town museum. I swam and I sunbathed. I became part of the landscape. I ate many leisurely meals with Mohi el Din. There was a dinner of little pigeons we had in a café under the trees by the river, there was a wedding party and Arab breakfasts. My social life took on its own momentum, propelling me from party to party in the good old way.

I was enjoying myself and if it hadn't been for Carole everything would have been fine. But Carole was a difficulty. I kept seeing her in the distance at cocktail parties or swimming at the club and the sight of that neat red hair and her clean cotton dresses made me long for my liberty. I wanted her hand in my hand and her smile across the table. But I couldn't let myself go near her outside office hours. Nor could I avoid her. I had to behave like what I was: a casual visitor on whom she had made no particular impression. In public I ignored her but in private, in my hotel room, I could not dismiss from my mind the things she had told me.

In private I was doing a despicable thing. I was reading every bit of paper I could find in Duncan's house. Each time I went there I came away with a briefcase stuffed full of his letters and notebooks, and whenever I had the chance I read and read and read. I read the letters from their sons, the household shopping book which the cook took to the suq every day, a collection of press cuttings, the visitors' book and Mrs Stuart's diaries. I left nothing untouched and when I had finished, I felt that I knew that family as if they were my own. Duncan Stuart was no longer a stranger but a man with whom I had walked and talked and become intimately acquainted. As for his wife, her endless complaints made me so miserable that I got drunk, just as he must have done night after night in that relentless oven of a town.

After my scrutiny I still wasn't sure that it had been necessary or that there was a murder waiting to be discovered, but I had come across some interesting bits and pieces.

The first concerned the missing cameras. It looked as if Duncan was having a spot of bother with the Ministry of the Interior over the renewal of his permit to film. It was forbidden to film or to take photographs outside the capital unless one had a permit. Usually there wasn't much trouble getting one. Duncan had had one for years and, since his only pleasure in life seemed to lie in taking photographs, he would indeed have been feeling persecuted if someone had deprived him of it. Everyone else had a licence, all the Embassy people. Even Batty had a licence. That reminded me that I didn't have one and I made up my mind to apply for one. Were they clamping down on all of us or was it just Duncan?

Duncan had been a competent man and his papers were beautifully kept. I found out that three times over the past ten months his house had been broken into and he had been robbed of small items, of cash that had been left lying around, of a Japanese tape recorder and an inexpensive camera belonging to his wife. He had made various claims on his insurance and had had the locks changed on his house. He suspected that a servant who he had sacked had taken copies of the keys.

From another insurance file I discovered that his wife had just taken out a lot more life insurance. She certainly hadn't been joking when she said she thought he would be killed. There wasn't a great of money involved but he had already been well covered and it seemed to me rather late in the day for a woman whose two sons were almost grown up to be taking out extra insurance. Duncan's pension would have been considerable by then, and it all looked very odd, unless of course she had been absolutely sure of getting her money back. That was the answer. She had been sure. As soon as I came across the correspondence I knew she had been sure, and not hysterical, either. She had been so sure that she had taken practical steps and invested some of her own capital against the event which Duncan either couldn't or wouldn't do anything to forestall. She hadn't expected that they would get her and the boys as well.

There was something though, something somebody had said which could explain it: she was terrified of planes. Now if Duncan's job had suddenly changed so that he would have to fly more than usual, that might have prompted the extra insurance. I checked in Duncan's office diary and found that he had made fewer flights into the desert lately than ever before. It couldn't have been aeroplanes, so it must have been something else. But what and when it had all started I just didn't know.

I tried to imagine myself in her place, a woman who was certain in her own mind that her husband was about to die. What other steps would I take? There was a blue file bulging with letters and receipts dealing with the letting of their house on the outskirts of Croydon. It was let on consecutive two-year leases; the Stuarts didn't always go there on leave because they loved the Arab world and would holiday in the Lebanon or Egypt whenever they had the chance. Before Damascus was put out of reach they used to go there. They were probably not very much at home in Croydon. The house had been re-let three months earlier but this time with a difference. Mrs Stuart who dealt with these things had written twice to her agent and asked him to insert an escape clause. If her husband's job in Arabia came to an end, she could now give the tenant a month's notice to leave, so that she would be able to go back and live there with her children should the need arise.

She was a careful woman, Mrs Stuart. But no more careful than dozens of other wives, neurotic whining women who cannot stand on their own feet and cling to their husbands with a desperation bordering on neurosis. Crazy? Was she unbalanced? The girls at the office thought so. It all depended on how you chose to view her dilemma. It became clear that I wasn't going to get any further unless I could find somebody who knew Mrs Stuart.

Joanna could have told me. I knew that. She was a shrewd judge of character. I bought an airletter form at the hotel reception desk and wrote to her. I could not write to her exactly because of the local censor but I did my best.

Dear J.

Did you ever get to know Janet Stuart? She is beginning to interest me. Do you happen to know what sort of things interested her? He, Duncan, seems to have been such a difficult person; everyone knows all about him. But what was she capable of? Anything?

I am hating it here. The heat is appalling as always and everything agonisingly slow. I can see that I shall be held up here for weeks. Nothing has changed. I wish so much I were with you all and not embarked on this grubby mission.

So many friends of yours send their love. I have told

them all how well you are and how happily settled now, which delights them. Your dear old house is still the same, don't worry. A man called Batty lives there now and his wife hasn't changed anything.

Love to you both and the children,

Mark

P.S. Bear is very well and sends his love to Judy. He is having a lovely time.

In fact I hadn't mentioned Joanna to anyone. There probably wasn't anyone left who would remember her. The years cover like sand out there and European faces disappear, arrive and disappear. We expatriates are the nomads of the world and even the Arabs accept it. No, Joanna was gone for good, gone from the suq, from her house, from the river, and all that remained of her in the whole country was the snapshot I carried in my pocket.

I didn't lie to her about her house though. It wasn't changed. The Battys were obviously people who accepted things as they found them which would have been a good thing, career-wise, under Duncan. Under Duncan. That was the trouble with them. They had been under Duncan and I had to meet not his underlings but her friends. Who might Mrs Stuart have confided in? Her diary was the place to look but it was a methodical and unenlightening book which documented her social engagements and her parties with guest lists and menus all complete so she would never offer anyone the same dishes twice. Why do I so hate these professional hostesses? I tried to analyse her engagements. They dined at the Residence and with the American Ambassador, too. They dined with anyone who was anyone in that town. But it was in the mornings that she would have been on her own and chosen her own companions. The initials S.S. cropped up at least once a week. There was also someone called P. who featured in her life rather erratically. She would see P. three or four times in a week and then for weeks together

P. would disappear. I didn't see how I was going to trace these people. At the back of the diary was a page for telephone numbers but she had listed the Embassy, the Doctor, and BOAC and the Office. There was no sign either of S.S. or of P. There were a lot of Arab and government telephone numbers noted down in her diary, which was queer.

I thought the best person to ask about S.S. was the one least likely to be suspicious, the least clever and the least complicated of the women I had met: Mrs Batty, that neat, mild-tempered little person who only came into her own on the tennis court. I got the car which had been hired for me out of the garage and drove round to see her while Peter was at work. It was very hot. The car was too hot to touch and bits of black plastic kept flaking off the steering wheel onto my sweaty hands. I felt very tired when I got to the house but at least I was out and doing something about the Stuart problem. I had had to drive through the suq at snail's pace so as not to mow down any donkeys or children and I was ready to come into the shade and have an iced beer. I remember I felt very free as I always feel when I get out of Europe and into shirt-sleeves. Life seemed good. I am glad it was that way because it turned out to be my last carefree ride.

Maybe I was already being followed but I didn't realise it. Otherwise I might not have intruded on Pauline Batty and her little world. Joanna's old house was nice although it was small, and in her living room there were windows open on three sides and a desert cooler to keep the air damp and fresh. Pauline was rather diffident when I said she could help me but she sent her cook-suffragi for a beer and sat down in a yellow armchair. I sat on another. The cover didn't look as if it had been cleaned since Joanna left. Everything near the desert gets dusty, parched and shabby, and that was how her living room was. But it was very comfortable and I felt comfortable with Pauline. Here was a woman who trusted me and was smiling at me calmly, just waiting for me to take my time and begin.

I said, 'Pauline, I have an idea and I think it's something you can help me with. The company magazine will be full of appreciations and obituaries of Duncan and I'd like his wife not to be neglected. I'm going to write something about her and I need help from her friends here.'

She understood exactly but she shook her head. 'I'm sorry but I didn't know Mrs Stuart at all well.'

'No?'

'She was always very kind. When we first arrived she gave me some empty gin bottles to store water in in the fridge. They're best she said because they are square and you can get more in . . . but no, I didn't know her.'

'Perhaps you can tell me who did know her?' I suggested.

'Well, I honestly don't know anything about her personal life. She liked jasmine, liked it very much. Sometimes when she came to a party here she would pick a bit of jasmine and pin it in her dress or in her hair. A bit old-fashioned to wear flowers but it smelt nice.'

'I think you can help me indirectly then. Mrs Stuart kept a list of her engagements (Pauline was sure to disapprove if I admitted to reading another woman's diary). She seems to have had a friend with the initials S.S. Have you any idea who that is?'

Pauline was so friendly and eager but she had no idea. I think she was conscious of having failed with one of her husband's superiors because she asked me to lunch, she pressed me to stay and said that her husband would probably know who S.S. was.

If I had wanted her husband and his colleagues to know that I was on the track of Mrs Stuart's lady friends, I wouldn't have come to ask Pauline. I tried again. 'Come on, I am sure we can do this between us. Whose surname begins with S? Tell me everyone in the place whose surname begins with S.'

She found a pencil and began to make a neat list which

grew to a dozen names before she was satisfied with it. Then she sat and looked at the list she had made.

'I've got it,' she said, pleased with herself at last. 'I know who it must be. It's Lady Silcox. Her name is Stella.'

Good God! I thought, because Lady Silcox was the wife of the British Ambassador.

'No other possibility?' I asked and then as I realised that any friendship with the Ambassador's wife would have been common knowledge, 'Was she great friends with Lady Silcox?'

'I didn't know she was,' said Pauline apologetically. 'Once a month I am supposed to go to the Residence for British Women's Circle tea parties and that's the only time I ever see Lady Silcox. Once Peter and I got asked to an ambassador's Queen's Birthday party when we were posted in the Gulf but here we get left out. We're too junior. Besides, the Embassy people keep themselves to themselves. They have all sorts of privileges,' she added wistfully.

'Can I use your phone?'

'Of course,' she said and led me through into a hallway beside the kitchen. Her cook was in there ironing Batty's shirts. He was a big black man with grizzled hair. He had taken off his turban and jallabiyah and was wearing his undershift, white shapeless cotton which fell to his knees. His feet were bare and his face was streaming with sweat. Seeing him at work I suddenly remembered him. He had been Joanna's servant. I ought to have greeted him in Arabic like an old friend and asked after his wife and children in the Sudan. But I rang up the Residence instead. On the telephone Lady Silcox had an upper-class English voice. She was politely mystified but, no, she had no engagements that morning. Yes, I could come round straight away if that was what I wished.

I did wish so I said goodbye to Pauline and went out to the car which was hotter than ever. I opened all the windows and took a couple of minutes to get her started. The garage had fobbed me off with an old battery. It's all those short journeys in the searing heat. So I was cursing the garage as I pulled out into the road and set off. And a car followed me.

Chapter Five

I WAS CONVINCED THAT it followed me. It was a battered yellow Mercedes taxi and it took every corner behind me. There were two Arabs in the front seats, both in European clothes. I went a round-about way to make sure it was me they were following. It was but I didn't try to lose them. El Aasima is too small a town to lose anyone for long and besides, if I was being followed, the Residence was the safest place I could be going. All residences have a police sentry, armed.

I comforted myself with that thought for the day as I swung the car round on the Residence drive and parked in the shade of its high garden wall. The policeman was leaning sleepily against his wooden sentry box and above his head the Union Jack waved lazily in the slight, hot breeze. I sat in the car for a minute and collected together every little item they might have tampered with. If they were going to put a bomb in my car, there was nothing I could do to prevent them. But I didn't think they would. Oil was so important. You can't kill off white oil men too indiscriminately. I would have to take it on trust that they had been told only to follow me and find out what I was doing with my time, whom I was seeing.

The street was empty. The yellow taxi drew up under the trees on the opposite verge and the doors were thrown open to try to dispel the heat. I hoped they would enjoy their wait. The policeman shifted his position and adjusted the little fez he wore with his khaki uniform. I rang the doorbell.

Suddenly I was nervous. The big white house with its imposing front door and uniformed servants was too much for me. I am not used to such surroundings and I wished that Janet Stuart had chosen someone else for her friend. I told myself that I was imagining difficulties. The wife of an ambassador is only the wife of a British civil servant and no more prone to airs and graces than any other middle-class English woman. Lady Silcox would probably turn out to be perfectly ordinary and easy and I would be able to find out all I wanted to know. If she had been Janet's friend perhaps she would be my friend too. If not, then I would have to readopt the obituary approach and behave as if I were interviewing her, *de bas en haut* as it were.

There is one great thing about the Residence. It is air conditioned throughout. Stepping into the tiled hall was like stepping into a cool sea. I bathed in the freshness. There was a Ministry of Works Lowry print on the wall and family portraits above the staircase up which I was now led to a most English-looking, light, chintzy drawing room. Lady Silcox was waiting for me and I could see at once how dicey it was going to be. She was a tall strong-looking woman with bobbed steel-grey hair and the same smart English voice I had heard on the telephone. She had a proud beak of a nose and because she was so tall she seemed to be looking down on me slightly, with disdain perhaps, certainly without any sympathy.

My quite futile reaction was to put my dark glasses back on. I felt crumpled and ignorant, as though I had been summoned by the headmistress. With great courtesy she advanced across the room, said what a pleasure it was to meet me and told me to sit down and let them bring me something to drink. As if on cue, I was brought the ubiquitous pistachios and fresh lemonade by two of her plump, contented servants. I could picture them having served successive British ambassadors for years. The Residence was probably the safest place in which to talk to anyone about murder. Our Ministry of Works would check it regularly for eavesdropping microphones.

'Well,' asked Lady Silcox. 'How can I help you, Mr Patterson?'

'I am interested in Janet Stuart. I believe you knew her well.'

'Yes,' she said. 'It's very tragic. We were all most horrified and upset.'

'I can understand that,' I said.

'I am going to miss her,' she told me and then she didn't say anything else but gazed at a photograph on the piano. It was an extremely beautiful picture of a young bride in white stockings and the white bridal clothes of the nineteen twenties marrying a British officer. She carried masses of lilies. It was with an effort that I dragged my attention back to Lady Silcox.

'Would it upset you to talk to me about Mrs Stuart?' I asked. 'I am here on behalf of her family and I feel that because of being abroad so long she had become rather remote from her relations, no longer quite real.'

'It happens to us all, Mr Patterson,' she retorted. 'I suppose,' she went on, still gazing at the family photograph, 'I suppose I could say without exaggerating that Janet Stuart was one of the cleverest women I have met. She was an old friend. We were up at Girton together. She got a first, not without effort, but she did get one. And she was so lucky being able to go on with her work even in this peripatetic life.'

'What sort of work was that?'

'Research. She completed many many studies of Arab village life. Too statistical to be easy reading for you and me perhaps, because she was extremely painstaking, extremely thorough in all she did. Lately she found it rather more difficult to go on field trips. Yes, she would have liked to go on more field trips.'

'I had no idea,' I said. 'No idea at all. Was her work published?'

'Oh, regularly, yes. She was an authority in her own small field. And lately there was a growing recognition of what she was doing. She was particularly interested in the changes that had been brought to bear on desert communities by the coming of the oil companies.'

'Rather an embarrassing subject for the wife of an oil man?'

'I think not. She passed no judgements. She was scientific in her approach and was content to record the facts. Her main interest used to be her children but when they went away to boarding school she became totally immersed in her economics again. I sometimes thought it must be a great blessing to have so much occupation in a post like this.'

A place where no one does anything unless they have to . . . for many wives in El Aasima the sole occupation is to endure the heat. How long and empty the mornings must seem without Janet to gossip with.

'I shall miss them all. Particularly in the holidays. Our children were roughly the same age, you see. They would swim together. Sometimes we would organise barbecues. Janet was good at organising.'

Lady Silcox herself must be no mean hand at organisation so this was high praise. I could tell from her expression that her opinion of me had sunk. I had totally failed to appreciate her friend. Could it be true that no one in Super Oil knew what a distinguished woman Mrs Stuart had been? I was astonished Janet Stuart wasn't just one of the wives. She had been somebody in her own right and if only I had had eyes to see, I could have guessed it from her photographs: a heavy-built, masculine woman with no-nonsense natural hair and a skin toughened and darkened by her time in the desert. A woman of courage who had gone alone into the remotest Arab villages and camps and then returned to the city, reluctantly put on a clean dress, combed her hair into some sort of order and gone out to dine with the managers and the sheikhs and the ambassadors her husband had collected. We hadn't appreciated that. We had had no notion.

'Lady Silcox,' I began, then I stopped in the middle of what I was saying.

'What can we do?' she asked.

By God, I knew it. I knew now exactly what was missing from Duncan's house. Nothing that had been inventoried or insured. Her papers. Every scrap of paper connected with her research. I had found nothing. I didn't know who had taken it. Another oil company, the Ministry of the Interior, the University . . . but it was all gone, what must have been a gold mine of information about the country.

'Lady Silcox,' I began again. 'I am not a fool. I misjudged Janet but I have been through all the Stuarts' possessions, getting them ready for the packers. There are no research papers there, nothing whatsoever to suggest that she was doing academic work of this sort.'

'I have copies of a few of her articles. There are other offprints in the Embassy library and I'm sure the University has some, too, if you're interested.'

She saw I hadn't meant to read them but she retrieved me with her habitual good manners. 'Is there anything else I can tell you, Mr Patterson? She was such a good friend of mine. I knew her very well . . . I wouldn't like . . .'

'There is something else, yes. I don't want to distress you but I feel you are the only person here who could give me a truthful answer, however unpleasant.'

'I don't understand,' she said.

'Some people have suggested that during the last few months Mrs Stuart was not quite herself. That she was, well, hysterical . . . on the verge of a nervous breakdown. Is there any truth in this?'

She hesitated. She was no fool, but I needed a straightforward answer before she had time to revert to training and become diplomatic.

'Some people,' I jogged her, 'were not so polite. They say she was already crazy. That she had gone mad.'

'You should not believe things people tell you, Mr Patterson. People here were not always kind to Janet. She was not exactly a pillar of the British community. There was no need for her to be and I didn't expect it of her. She was in some ways an eccentric. She was not mad unless you believe it mad to go off to the desert with notebooks and tape recorder, and to prefer the company of Arabs to that of the English.'

I laughed and she laughed too, thereby excluding all the philistine British who fill commercial posts in the Arab world.

'And the last few months? She was not distressed?'

'Yes, I think she was distressed. She was unhappy but not hysterical. She was perfectly able to deal with her problems.'

'What sort of problems, Lady Silcox?'

'I think she and Duncan were worried about their future in the Arab world, about his future in the company. They felt that he had probably got as far as he could go and there was not much ahead of him. But you probably know far more about that than I do.'

No, no, I didn't. There was only one thing I knew which she didn't and I decided to tell her. But before I could do so she exclaimed, 'People aren't suggesting that Janet committed suicide are they? You know, "while the balance of her mind was disturbed"?' With what utter derision she spoke; with what confidence in her own judgement.

I shook my head. 'It's a possibility but a very remote possibility. No, there's another reason why I'm not happy about the situation. Apparently Janet, Mrs Stuart, told one or two people that her husband was being victimised. By someone. We don't know who. She even thought they might go as far as to kill him. Did she ever mention this to you?'

Looking very shocked, Lady Silcox shook her head. 'No, not at all.'

'That's why I'm anxious to find out whether she was mentally stable when she died. If she was, then we ought to take her fears seriously.'

'Certainly we ought if she did say these things. But she never mentioned it to me and I'm inclined to doubt it.'

Lady Silcox had been sipping a glass of plain water. Now she put it down on the tray and walked across the room. Her dress was cut away at the back like the dress of a younger woman and I could see the moles and muscles of her back, the details of her skin, as she stood with her back to me looking out of the window.

After a long time she turned round. 'There is one thing. Something my husband noticed. We were in Aden during the troubles. And there were certain precautions staff were expected to take. We were asked to remove the hub caps on our cars because it was possible for a terrorist to put explosive in behind them. My husband noticed one evening that Duncan and Janet were driving their Jaguar without the hub caps and I'm afraid my husband made a sick joke about it later on when we got home. I always assumed they'd been stolen.'

Odd how diplomats can come to know things we workers never dream of. I felt angry. Angry with the world and myself and my suspicions.

I said, 'I must ask you not to mention what I have said to you. Naturally, as soon as I have any evidence I shall get in touch with the police and possibly with the Consul too. But until then I think it best to be discreet.'

'I quite agree,' she said.

'One last question. If Janet thought that she was in danger and her husband, too, do you think she would have confided in you?' She gave me a hard look. She was not a slight woman but at times her face looked gaunt, very very hard with the hardness of the hereditary aristocrat. What a question to ask her.

'We confided in each other,' she said objectively. 'We were good friends. There are things I imagine I would not have confided in Janet . . . Embassy matters, political matters if I had known of any. I think it possible that she too might have shown discretion. If for instance Duncan had become involved in local politics. My husband is, after all, British Ambassador. If she considered it might embarrass me . . . it might involve us . . . That is the only situation I can conceive of, Mr Patterson.'

I stood up. Outside a sprinkler was twirling on the long Embassy lawns. Bright bougainvillea overhung the trellis round the little blue swimming pool. I did not want to go. I loved her house. I loved even her haughtiness. I loved the way she played by the rules because in my world that didn't happen.

Chapter Six

WHEN I GOT OUT to the car the yellow taxi was still parked under the trees waiting for me. It escorted me sedately back towards the hotel but I had something else to do first. I turned left and drove to Duncan's house where Ali was stretched out on his angareeb in the shade in a midday stupor. I didn't disturb him but walked round to the garage which was built onto the side of the house. I had sold Janet Stuart's little Fiat and the garage was empty. I hadn't bothered with the garage before. Now I went quickly to the far end and found what I was looking for. Stacked neatly in the corner were the hub caps. Eight hub caps, four from each car. I just stood and looked. That was the worst of all.

Ali caught me like that, the bastard. He always caught me unprepared. I don't know what he thought I was doing in the garage. There were no secrets there, but he made a habit of overdoing things. This time he didn't come quite so close to killing me but I was furious with him, quite ridiculously furious. He was after all only doing his job but I had been unnerved by the men on my tail and by now I was certain that Duncan had not just died. He and his family had been murdered in cold blood and, what was more terrible, Duncan himself had been aware all along that it was going to happen.

So while I raged and stormed at Ali I was really raging at Duncan, cursing him for his courage and his pig-headedness and his failure to tell any of us what was happening to him. I left the house in a fury and almost forgot to notice that the taxi had gone. Maybe the driver had knocked off for lunch. I needed to retreat to the hotel and think everything out again and I needed someone to talk to over my beer. I was in no frame of mind to keep to the rules and I decided that the person I needed was Carole.

When I had the idea of calling on Carole it was because I needed to explain how I felt about the murder. Other girls in the block probably thought I wanted to sleep with my secretary. Well, I did, but that was the least of what I hoped for from Carole. Only she had seen fit to transmit the warning from Janet Stuart and I wanted to tell her that I now believed her. I needed to offload my anger; one always needs someone to blame for a death.

We take flats for our secretaries in a European-style block near the town centre. There are no lifts and the stairways are of unadorned concrete carpeted with a film of sand that blows in from the desert, but once through her front door a girl can feel at home. Carole welcomed me. Indeed I got the feeling that she had been waiting for me for she pulled out a chair ready and put out a hand to take my jacket.

'I'm filthy,' I warned her. 'Don't touch me.' I was dusty from that lunatic's garage.

'Take a shower if you like.' She nodded towards the bathroom. Her living room was decorated with souvenirs of her posting in Hong Kong. There were frail Chinese prints of blossom and birds. Everything was like its owner, clean and bright. It would have been unpardonable to talk of murder at that moment. She did not want to talk about it. She made that very clear. She found some cigarettes and said she would tell Mohammed I was staying for lunch.

I showered as she suggested but it was so hot even in the flat that I went on sweating and couldn't get dry again afterwards. My clothes stuck to my legs. My head ached.

She brought me beer but I drank a glass of salt water instead. I loathe the taste of the stuff, but I knew that if I didn't drink it I'd feel worse before the day was over. Then the beer.

'How's the tennis?' I asked her. I had heard that she and Pauline Batty were likely to win the women's doubles at the club.

'You think it's silly, all my tennis, don't you?' she laughed. 'Oh well . . . ' She shrugged and her long thin arms and legs all became part of the shrug.

'So long as you're happy here.'

'Of course. I couldn't live without the sun. Think of English winters!'

I walked towards the window and noted that there was a black taxi parked a little way along the road. The men who had waited outside the Residence were waiting again. Carole went on talking about how she loved the tropics and parties and always being out of doors. But I went to the telephone and dialled the Ministry of Petroleum Affairs. It wasn't yet two o'clock and they didn't go home for lunch till two.

'Mohi el Din?' We exchanged the courtesies. 'Look,' I said, 'if you can spare a moment on your way home to lunch, just drop round here. I'm at Flat 9 in the Allawah Building opposite that big chemists on the corner of the square. You know it?'

He said he did.

'There are two men who have been following me in taxis all morning. I want to know who they are. If they're your people, you can call them off. I'm straight with you and in any case I'm not going to make off for London. I'll get an exit visa before I go and come and say goodbye.'

'They're not government men, Mark. We wouldn't do a thing like that to you. And if we did, we wouldn't let you see it, not after only one morning.'

'Oh, they want me to see them all right. That's why they're there. They want to frighten me off, and they're succeeding.'

'I'll be round,' he promised.

Carole had lit a cigarette. 'So you're being tailed?' she said.

'I think so.'

'Why on earth?'

'Why was Duncan murdered?'

'Oh,' she said, 'that joke's sick. Forget I ever said it.'

I looked down at my shoes, desert boots all yellowish white with dust. 'I think he was murdered only I don't have any material proof. I have got to have something absolutely concrete to prove it when I go and challenge the police . . . and I don't see that I've got any hope of coming up with anything.'

'Who murdered him?' she asked. She was very attractive but not intelligent. How she thought I knew who had done it when I couldn't even prove that it had been done . . .

'I'm not a detective,' I snapped. 'I don't know who did it. I don't know if it was an American who paid an Arab to do it or an Arab who paid an Englishman.' I didn't know if it was in the oil business, or local politics, or just Duncan the man who had been for the chop.

She coloured up when I snubbed her but she said with great patience, 'What I meant was that, if you could discover who killed him, that would be all you needed to go to the police.'

'Any suggestions as to how I do that?'

She went to the window then and looked down on the taxi. 'You don't have far to go,' she said, 'if they're waiting for you down there.'

If I had been a hero I would have leaped for the stairs at that moment. But I am not a hero and she was joking; she had to be joking. Besides, there was no indication that either of those men in their cheap Italian-cut suits and mesh sandals had had anything to do with the fire in which Duncan had died. For that matter who had? There must have been a bomb.

Someone had placed a bomb, almost certainly. Probably a home-made bomb contrived from aluminium shavings. It hadn't gone off at once, so he hadn't linked it to the ignition. It must have been triggered off by the differential and then set the car ablaze with its own petrol. Someone had wired the bomb up at the airport while the car had been left in the car park. The place was unwatched and sometimes deserted. There was no water at hand, so the Arab boys who haunt other car parks never came there to pick up a few piastres washing cars. A driver could have done it . . . a chauffeur or a taxi driver just waiting . . . not a European though, because Europeans do not tinker with cars in the hot afternoon sun out at the airport. The Arabs do. They belong to a different world: the third world. They come and go and drive and contrive just as we tell them. Poor bastards, who can blame them if they kill one of us every now and then to even things up a little? No, you can't blame them.

But that wasn't how it happened to Duncan, was it? It wasn't one spontaneous, glorious gesture of defiance that polished him off. In his case it had been cold, premeditated murder. It had been part of a plan and he had known all about it. The people who had murdered Duncan had tortured him first, and I didn't think I cared to approach them with a friendly gesture on the deserted street while the rest of the population ate its lunch and took its regular siesta.

'Tell me about Mr Stuart,' I said to her. 'What sort of a man was he?' I didn't tell her I had met Duncan and disliked him. I left her to pick her own words, her own way of remembering her boss.

She smiled at me then and it was not difficult to see that she enjoyed remembering. 'He had fair hair,' she began. 'He was handsome. He tanned brown in the sun, not brick-red like most others, and his eyes were very blue.'

'What was he like to work for?'

'A gentleman; always considerate, always making things easy for me. For instance, just small things in the office. He wouldn't have me hang onto the phone for him or monitor his calls. He took care of little things for himself so I could press on with the typing if there was a lot to do.' I could see she was still a bit in love with him. 'I don't think I'll like staying on here to work for somebody else,' she confessed.

'He talked to me as if I were his daughter . . . I suppose it never occurred to him that I was much too old.'

'Did he ask you to his house?'

'No, only at Christmas when he had all the staff. No, it wasn't that sort of relationship. He was strict. He was an old-fashioned man and life outside the office didn't seem to count for him. He wanted the work done, and done quickly. It never entered his mind that I might have had a game of tennis fixed on the evenings he suddenly asked me to stay late.'

'But you stayed?'

'One had to. For him. He worked long hours.'

She didn't have to tell me that. Duncan overworked and refused to delegate. His girls usually fretted and wept because he drove them so hard. I'd have treated her better than he but she wouldn't have loved me for it in the way she had loved him. Not that she had really liked him in the way she liked me and those young American marines with whom she spent days on the river and evenings dancing. It was more that she had owned Duncan. He had been hers to look after and to organise. The fact that he was a busy man and an important man made her busy and important, too. Who could resist such a position in one of our humdrum offices? When he died she suddenly lost her status and if I hadn't come she would have been hanging around still with no particular role. But I had come and she was now helping me just as she had helped Duncan. She was telling me all the things she thought I wanted her to say and I didn't believe more than half of them. As far as I was concerned she was a good secretary but she was better at home and that was why I was sitting down with her to eat when Mohi el Din rang the bell.

We gave him a drink and pressed him to eat, too. There was enough food for all of us. With Arab cooks there is always enough food; it is a matter of honour. Mohammed would nip up the back stairs and borrow from one of the other cooks rather than let guests go short.

He had produced a curry for us. It was not the aromatic meat the Arabs eat cooked with saffron and cardamom and chick peas. Nor was it a recognisable Indian curry. It was what we always got from our Arab cooks: a British officers' mess curry made with a tin of curry powder from London. But the unpretentious curries eaten by the British in El Aasima are only the foundation for a feast of other things. So the curry prepared for Carole became the centre-piece of a vast meal. Mohammed brought side-dishes of hard-boiled eggs, bananas, tomatoes, crushed peanuts, home-made mango chutney, coconut and mounds of white rice which was imported, at great expense, from the United States. Occasionally the Armenian shops ran out of this rice; it was a political barometer which showed when the government was swinging to the left.

While we ate, Mohi el Din regaled us with his best stories about oil men in the desert and drank three cans of iced beer. Even the sight of the men waiting for me would not persuade him that anything unpleasant was going on. That side of life had hardly touched Mohi el Din.

'I'll have a word with them, if you want,' he said grudgingly, 'but what can I say? I'd rather see for myself. We could go for a drive in your car and carry out a little experiment.'

I made no move to get up. I felt ready for an afternoon sleep and wished that he had not other ideas. For when Mohi el Din has ideas I know from experience that other people fall in with them. He has great energy and charm. When he smiles, his teeth flash white and he is irresistible.

'Come on, old man. I will take you both to see the pelicans on the river.'

Carole looked at me questioningly.

'You'll like that,' he told her.

Carole nodded and went to get her sunglasses and camera. There didn't seem to be much against an afternoon's sight-seeing so I got ready, too, and we trooped down the dark concrete stairs and into the appalling brightness of the afternoon.

The sound of wailing Arab music on Radio Cairo came to us from the waiting taxi but Mohi el Din admitted as he held out his hand for the car keys that he did not recognise the two men waiting there. I had no hope that Carole would recognise them for she was patently one of those Europeans to whom all Arabs look alike. Once, I suppose, that had been true of me, too. It comes as a shock to a liberal Englishman to find that when the Arab police wish you to identify a man they start off by asking his height and the colour of his skin. Colour is significant in El Aasima; it should be noted and remembered.

They were the same men as that morning but driving a different car. The elder had that pale skin they call olive, though I am not sure why. The other was slightly darker. Neither was as dark as Mohi el Din and this surprised me because, more often that not, a man's colour is some guide to his social class. One or two government ministers could have passed for Italians but many of the labourers on building sites were as black as Negroes. I discriminate between them because discrimination is sadly acceptable out there and rich, clever men choose pale-skinned girls to be their brides. Actually the marriages are arranged by their families but it all boils down to the same thing.

Mohi el Din was helping a smiling Carole into the back of the car. I thought that if my redoubtable parents had picked my girl for me, I might still have been married and safely established in my own domestic box instead of taking up with leggy red-headed girls from the office. I could not understand why she was happy to photograph pelicans in the middle of a murder hunt. How delicious she looked. With what aplomb she settled onto the scorching hot seat of the car. I'd not looked at other girls since I met her. She was always posed as if for a glossy advertisement . . . white sandals, long freckled legs, white dress, a sweet freckled face and the urchin red hair. That afternoon for the drive she had put on enormous sunglasses and a floppy white hat. It was an English garden-party hat, a hat for a wedding in one of those mock Tudor villages the other side of Windsor. Joanna had once worn a hat like that.

As we took our seats I asked Mohi el Din if he remembered Joanna. I knew he must because Robert and he had been good friends and Joanna had even got as far as paying a call on Mohi el Din's hidden wife. Hadn't he even spent a weekend with Robert and Joanna while he had been in England for a training course? Mohi el Din fitted the key into the unfamiliar ignition and started the engine before answering, no, he didn't remember Joanna. Robert, yes, he would have met anyway through the Ministry, but it was a long time ago and he had forgotten Joanna.

Arabs do not lie to their friends. They have a more discreet habit, though, of giving the answer that will not give offence, the answer they believe you would like to hear. Maybe Mohi el Din figured that Robert's day was over and that I would find it more convenient to have him out of the way, well forgotten.

'I was staying with them before I came out here,' I told him. 'They loved your country, you know, they loved El Aasima. Joanna would enjoy this ride by the river. I'll write and tell her all about it.'

I was thinking, Acknowledge her, you bastard, why won't you acknowledge her now you know I'm her friend? But he didn't, and because I liked him I had to assume that he genuinely had forgotten. The hunting trips he took them on, the desert holidays and long meals at Arab restaurants in the open air down by the river or in the shadow of the Catholic church in town were erased, erased from his life as they had been from Robert's and Joanna's. I thought I'd send Joanna a postcard and one for the children too, of camels perhaps and a Bedouin tent. They now sold postcards at the hotel and at the General Stores but I could remember a time when you couldn't buy picture postcards in El Aasima. There were none and there were no tourists to buy them, nor mere travellers. Only the occasional real explorer who stopped in the town to provision himself for his trek.

I would write,

'Dear Joanna, You remember Mohi el Din? He took me down the river to see the pelican colony by the island there . . .' That was what I thought I would write before Mohi el Din set off. Once he got the gears sorted out, he drove with total assurance and at a speed which left me quivering. You could tell it was his native town and that he was a favoured son. Chicken-sellers, urchins, sheep, every man and beast that valued its life scattered from our path; Mohi el Din assumed that they would and could. He kept one hand pressed on the horn and trusted to that. We sped down a shabby shopping street where old Italians left stranded by the Second World War sell coffee and iron-mongery, then on past the Arab bakeries and brothels (small queues, here, which suddenly dissolved against the house sides as we charged like a tank through their harmless afternoon). When we emerged on the parade ground in front of the Palace I knew from the way Mohi el Din kept glancing up at the mirror that we were being followed once more.

'We'll throw them off,' he assured me. 'We'll show them.' He took the avenue through the old palace gates where there is now a public park and ignoring the speed limit he only just managed to turn, skidding, onto the river bank road. Through more big wrought-iron gates we left the palace grounds and raced with glorious unconcern along the water side. Mohi el Din was enjoying himself.

'Enough,' I said. 'Enough. Let's go back.'

I thought that at least we might take Carole home and get her out of this, but I suspect that for Mohi el Din half the fun would have gone out of it had Carole not been there.

We now left the narrow alleys of the old town and came to areas I had never known, places that were marked 'Class 4 Workers' Housing' on the municipal grid. There were acres of identical streets with little sunbaked mud houses which we seemed to clear by inches. I was afraid we would kill a child playing outside, or a goat that had been left loose to forage on cardboard boxes. Mohi el Din with his aristocratic blood might get away with it, but as a foreigner I knew there would be short shrift for me in any accident. The black taxi seemed to slide along behind us and at last I began to take the chase seriously. I was menaced now by something I did not understand. I could not understand how I had overstepped the mark and involved myself in an Arab underworld I had never met before. Mohi el Din's driving, which was cavalier at the best of times, now had me gripping the seat.

'Go to the police station,' I shouted above the engine noise.

'And spoil the game?' he asked.

'It's no game.'

'I promise you, you'll be all right. While you are with me you will be fine,' he said. He brought us out of the maze of houses into the camel market where there are Egyptian political slogans splashed across the crumbling mud walls. In the heat of the afternoon no trading was going on. Only in the camel park a sleepy boy kept watch on the hobbled animals left there. The camels themselves had folded their legs and sunk in rest on the sunbaked earth. Beyond the camel park was the desert and before I realised what was happening we were heading for the wilderness with Mohi el Din whistling at the wheel.

It was mad. It was quite mad what he was doing. We didn't have much petrol and the car wasn't fit for the desert. The battery had been worrying me and in any case one needs heavy-duty suspension to survive the ruts and corrugations of a desert track. Land-Rovers crossed the desert, and camels laden with firewood, and swaying suq lorries piled high with a cargo of goods and people. But that was all. Not a down-in-the-mouth saloon car with no water or petrol on board and not even a compass to drive by.

'The car won't take it,' I shouted, but he brushed me aside and turned, grinning to Carole, 'No, now we've started we must finish them off.'

He was right. There was only one road going this way and with the taxi behind us we couldn't turn back. We had to go on.

'I don't like it,' I shouted. There was no knowing where we would end up.

'I know a way back. There is another track which the donkeys sometimes use. Behind the graveyard in the fold of that first wadi.'

'How does one get onto it from here?'

'At the next village. You'll see.'

Once in the desert Mohi el Din was on his own ground. He handled the car as one handles a flying horse. We left the last buildings. The road was a road no longer, just an expanse of corrugated tyre tracks stretching into the distance. For a mile or two there was acacia scrub and then nothing but sand and stones. The desert deceives the eye with an emptiness. We saw nothing but the circle of the horizon and the blue dome of the sky.

Mohi el Din's hands shook on the shuddering steering wheel as he struggled to keep control. The sweat ran down his face. His white European shirt clung to his streaming body. He drove fast and we held on for dear life.

Carole's knuckles showed white as she gripped the back of my seat. I wished I were sitting beside her so I could have put my arm round her and reassured her. I could not reach her but I took her hand instead and held that.

'Why so fast?' she mouthed at me.

'It's worse if you go slowly,' I shouted back. The only tolerable way to drive these roads is fast. Go slowly and the car will shake to pieces on the corrugations. Gather speed and the tyres start to skim the tops of the indentations. Mohi el Din drove like that, so we seemed to float on the dust. I knew we were skidding. It was like breasting a sea at high speed but he kept the car on the road. He knew what he was doing. He was laughing. He was enjoying himself.

'You'll not lose them out here,' I said. 'They can see where we are.' For we were raising a golden wake of dust that hung like a cloud over the road behind us. In the desert it is easy to follow, as the ancient Hebrews did, the pillar of dust.

'Are they still there?' he asked me.

'Yes. I think so.' At times through the dust it seemed as though I could see in the far distance another burst of dust which was the taxi struggling to follow us.

'We're mad,' I said. 'What do we do if we get stuck in the sand? We've no sand tracks to help us get free. And what do we do if they catch up? We've no guns.'

'Are they armed?' he asked quickly.

'I've no idea.'

'You don't trust me, Mark,' he said.

I thought bitterly that I had trusted him and that was the trouble. I had handed over the car keys and he had embarked on this crazy chase which was getting me absolutely nowhere and was scaring Carole out of her wits. She was clinging so tightly to my arm that her rings were hurting me. I knew that after this accidental closeness we'd not be able to go back to our old relationship. Her grey eyes, fixed trustingly on mine, were non-committal but I knew that the barrier between us was down.

I smiled back at Carole and she smiled too. It was, now we were really clear of the town, quite nice in the desert. Carole had probably never been there before. One can live for years in El Aasima and never set foot in the real Arabia. I don't know what it is that keeps the English penned in their own club and their own houses. Indolence, ignorance, perhaps. Or fear, I suppose, because deserts are fearsome places which demand respect, just as high mountains do. A man can die in the desert without anyone knowing why or how. I was glad that Carole had begun to like it but I was also thankful for her frivolous hat and her ridiculous white dress, which was now covered with fine grains of brown sand. She didn't look as if she was about to die.

'What are we doing?' she wanted to know. She might well ask. I hadn't wanted a car chase. There was not, when I came to think of it, much point in throwing off our pursuers. What I had wanted at lunchtime was to find out who they were and what they wanted of me. I had imagined that they might have wanted something of Duncan and this thing might have led them to kill him. That was why I had rung Mohi el Din, and instead of helping me to talk to these people he was making it look as though I was running away from them. He was intent on putting as much distance between us as possible.

After about an hour in the desert we came to a village I had not seen before. The track crossed a couple of dried-up wadis and bore off to the left. Soon a pathetic group of houses gradually became clear on the skyline. They were yellow and brown like the desert and were deeply shadowed on the northern side. They looked like children's bricks scattered on the sand.

Carole leaned forward to see and could not help saying 'How lovely!' because from far off that little ochre and terracotta village did look picturesque. It wasn't so pretty close up. It was one of the usual places with crumbling mud houses and a rough thorn zariba for the animals. Apart from a few goats there was no movement in the village. Two women were coming up from the well in the distance with a jerrycan of water. A bit of dirty rag lay in the road. Mohi el Din turned up a side alley and stopped the car in the shade.

I wanted to press on, but he shook his head, and we got out.

'We'll wait for them here,' he said.

'Are they armed?' It was my turn to ask.

He shrugged. 'You don't need to worry. These are my people.' I took him to mean that this village belonged to men of his tribe who would take our side in any quarrel. I hoped he was right.

'Keep back against the wall,' he said. 'They'll miss us.'

I pushed Carole behind me. So, cramped together, we waited. It wasn't for long. The taxi had matched our speed and was hurtling towards us. Its driver made no allowances for the lie of the land. As he reached the wadi by the village, a rough stream-bed where the water carves out its own course when the rare rains come, he ploughed straight through the debris of stone. Rocking wildly the taxi ran onto the firm ground within the village. They would have continued out the other side and landed up I know not where in the emptiness beyond had not one of them noticed our tyre marks. He grabbed the wheel from the driver and the taxi turned sharply towards us. It sailed sideways on the loose dust, hit a bucket, then a wall and then, so quickly it was difficult to get out of its way, it flew round and crashed horribly into the only tree in the place. I thought the tree would fall and crush the car but it didn't. It was the car that caved in at the front. Its bonnet reared up and the noise all stopped.

We stood and watched the drama as if it had been laid on especially for us. I put my arm round Carole's shoulder and through the thin cotton of the dress could feel her still trembling from the vibration of the car. We were all of us unsteady on our feet and made no effort at all to help the men from the broken taxi. I think that for one primitive moment I hoped that it would burst into flames and the Arabs would disappear as Duncan had disappeared in, a blaze of petrol. That would have been freak justice for him.

It was an Arab who ran across and seized the door handle, one of the villagers with a dirty blue and white check cloth wound roughly round his head. Men and children had appeared from all sides and stood at a respectful distance in a circle round the wrecked taxi. It took three men to force its door open and two familiar figures struggled out of the crushed interior. They must have survived by some miracle for they seemed stunned but unhurt. It was the shock which made them stagger in circles like blind men. The villagers watched and did nothing. They drew back as I had drawn back.

Mohi el Din, on the other hand, burst out laughing. At first I thought he must be suffering from shock too but as the laughter spread among the watching Arabs I saw that he was laughing at his victory. He was rubbing salt in their hurt: that humiliation which is anathema to an Arab. Half-bewildered, half-belligerent, the two men were trapped in a circle of laughing villagers. There was nothing they could do.

I took my chance. I unhooked Carole's camera from round her neck and took some photographs. If those men got hold of another taxi back in the city and tried to start the whole game again I would like to have their pictures to show the police.

'Come on,' said Mohi el Din, 'come on. Let's go.' He knocked my hand on the camera, and it fell to the ground. Immediately he bent to pick it up but I got there first. It looked unbroken. The lens was not cracked. To make sure I decided to take a picture of Carole too. She was standing among a group of curious villagers but she was as calm and still as a Madonna in an oil painting. I suppose that was what attracted me. I had never seen Carole alarmed or even moved. Her white arms and face were streaked with brown dust and with sweat but, if she noticed, she didn't seem to mind; she took the good and bad alike with neutrality. When her camera fell she watched with flat detachment. If we had ever got as far as visiting the pelicans she would have watched them in exactly the same way. I liked her for it.

It would be good to get back to the town and have a shower and some cold beer and then sit with Carole on the hotel terrace while the world walked by.

'Come on,' said Mohi el Din. 'I'm not waiting here for the police.'

I didn't think there was much chance of meeting up with the police out there but there was a telephone link to the village and Mohi el Din knew the local people better than I did.

'You shouldn't have photographed them,' he said in the car. 'These people are uneducated. If you photograph them they take offence.'

'I'm sorry,' I said. I knew that he would never apologise and one of us had to.

He was still grinning when we got back to the town. He brought us in round the cemetery with its tattered cairns and graves and then back to the zaribas of the animal market. The patient camels were still lying there hobbled nose to foot with their heavy packs laid out on the sand beside them.

Slowly, sleepily, the town had woken up. Nightshirted children ran up to the car, calling to us for backsheesh and cigarettes. Mohi el Din threw them a packet. We were back and we were alive, but looking at the children scrapping for those cigarettes, I felt very foreign at that moment.

Chapter Seven

OFFICE HOURS ARE OFFICE hours even in Arabia and I was too much conditioned by my organisation to evade them. So the time I had hoped to have alone with Carole in her flat, I spent in isolation going through Duncan's files in the office.

The oil business bites two ways. Until the North Sea turns up trumps, Europe needs the oil from the desert and the Arabs need the revenue it brings in. How much? is the question. It isn't just a question of how much in royalties and long negotiations with OPEC, the Organisation of Petroleum Exporting Countries. There's the question of how much investment too. As an oil company we have to prospect for oil and we have to show a profit from the oil wells once we have drilled them. We have to have pipelines to the coast and safe tanker terminals where we can get the crude on board. A production company needs experts and organisers on the spot and that still means employing expatriates. Expatriates mean friction with the local people who think the Europeans are getting all the cream.

By Arab standards they are. Europeans demand the food they are used to, medical care, swimming pools and alcohol if we can manage it. To reassert their own sovereignty the Arabs insist that expatriates also have Residence Permits, Work Permits, Visas, Export and Import Permits and Driving Licences. I am responsible for all this red tape and white paper which drives me up the wall. And while these frustrating minutae are being ground fine and small by the various Arab ministries which deal with them, there remain the long-term prospects and problems which Duncan had always handled so very well.

I'd examined all his papers and they only confirmed what London already knew: that Duncan was masterly at getting on with Arabs who mattered. Negotiations for the future had been going very well. I didn't come across any major point of difference that could have led to Duncan's death. Of course the Arabs always want more money than is realistic and we perhaps would like to give them less than they deserve, but in the end we come to an agreement. We have to. I was becoming convinced that oil interests alone had not led to Duncan's death.

Yet it had been the Arabs who did for him. It had all the marks of a terrorist murder. There were politics behind it. Otherwise how could I explain the missing travel permits, the official clampdown on Duncan's photographs? Somehow I had to explain why those two men had followed me. Because I was an oil man? Or because I was a friend of Duncan's? There are oil men all over Arabia and none but Duncan had been murdered. So the only explanation was that he, he personally, had done something to annoy an Arab. Yet that was unlikely because Duncan had nothing to do with the Arabs on our payroll. For technical matters he would employ Europeans, if he had to, but for hiring and firing, whether of clerks or draughtsmen or labourers, he had Arab personnel managers in charge. The government liked us to have local people in these jobs but we did it for our own benefit too. It worked better that way. The younger generation of some of the best families in the country worked for us and the Arabs under them accepted their authority without question because it was an allegiance which came naturally, part of the social fabric of the old Arab world.

Mohi el Din was one of these sheikhly men who were born to command. He frightened me. He would have had no hand in murdering Duncan but he was trying to cover up for someone. When he knocked the camera out of my hand he was telling me to stop. His violent driving had been a reminder that he was my master. At a word from him, my visa would be withdrawn and I would be packed onto the first plane back to London.

I drew a date palm on my notepad and wondered where in the country was an Arab who would benefit from Duncan's death. None of the sheikhs who were his friends. But there are others more prickly and more significant if one has an eye to the future: men who have started off in the oil companies straight from school as nothing in particular, and through their own knowledge and ingenuity have eventually risen to take charge. We had one of these new men. His name was Fahd Mohammed Ahmed. He didn't know about computers but he could organise anything from an office to a new road. In fact he was building a road at that moment which was why I'd only managed to speak to him over a crackling telephone line. It was a pity that, because Fahd made it his business to know all the men who worked for us and there was little you could hide from him. He knew the men and he knew the machines. One day he'll be put up for a training course in the States and he'll come home knowing all about computers too. The way I see it, that's what's going to happen. Whatever London do about replacing Duncan, sooner or later it will be Fahd who's manager of the production company. If this country ever gets too hot for Europeans to handle (and it was much too hot for Duncan) then Fahd will be our man in El Aasima.

I finished drawing in the leaves of the palm tree and wondered idly whether he might have tried to hurry things up a little by pushing Duncan out of his way.

I was still thinking about Fahd when suddenly Peter Batty, red-faced and sweating, came charging in the door shouting that we had got to get the police. There is something incredibly comic about a hot, fat, propertied Englishman shouting for the police in a foreign country where the police have more popular tasks than protecting expatriates.

'Shut up, man,' I snapped at him, 'and tell me what's the matter.'

He stopped shouting and began to talk. Over his shoulder I could see Carole palely hovering in the background. If this is a long story, I thought, then it's goodbye to that long, luxurious evening with Carole that I'd promised myself when we were out in the desert and she had clung to me for support.

Batty sat down and mopped his face. 'I've got to get home to Pauline,' he panted. 'They've broken into my house . . . '

It was the usual story. The husband is at work. The wife out shopping, the servant has finished work for the day and it's the hour of the petty thief.

'O.K. Go on home,' I said irritably, thinking that at least he'd leave Carole behind. Foolishly I asked, 'Do you want me to come to the police station with you?'

I expected the answer no because even with his minimal Arabic he ought to have been able to handle this sort of thing for himself. But he said yes and afterwards I was glad of it because his burglary wasn't the usual story after all. Pauline Batty hadn't gone out shopping. It was more complicated than that.

As I sat in Batty's car, I noticed with something like resignation that I was being followed once more. It was two fresh faces after that afternoon but they grinned at me as if we were conspirators together in some enormous joke. I wasn't amused. I did laugh though when we got to the Battys' house for there was his cook, peaceful Hassan, sitting in one of the plastic garden chairs on the veranda with Pauline's largest, sharpest kitchen knife resting on his knees. He looked petrified.

'Pauline's expecting a baby,' Batty whispered. 'She mustn't be upset. I can't have her being upset like this.'

When she heard the car she came out on the veranda to meet us and, though she was put out by what had happened, she didn't seem particularly upset. But she was pregnant so I had to be careful. In fact that was part of the story. It was early days yet and no one knew about the baby except her husband but quietly and without making a fuss she had begun to take care of herself and the child within her. That afternoon the house ought to have been empty; Pauline always used to spend Tuesday afternoons down at the club playing in their weekly informal tennis tournament. But now she was pregnant she stayed at home and rested instead. Peter had been playing tennis as usual. I had been out in the desert. Mohi el Din had seen to that. Pauline had shut the bedroom door, closed the shutters, turned on the air conditioner which drowned all other noise and gone to sleep. At four o'clock she woke up, dressed and made herself a pot of china tea. Then she settled down with a book on the sofa and waited for her husband to get back from work.

She was reading when the bell rang. The bell was at the front gate on the other side of the little garden. It was rare for it to ring because hawkers came to the kitchen window and friends usually walked straight in. She got to her feet, slipped on her wooden sandals and clopped across the garden to see who was there.

At the gate was an Arab in a neat white turban, not a headcloth, and because he spoke no English she did not understand him very well. She thought that he wanted to speak to Peter and she explained that he was at the office. But she was a girl to whom all the common politeness of life came naturally, as naturally as to the Arabs among whom she lived. She invited the man to come in and wait on the veranda until her husband arrived back.

The man went on talking in Arabic and she gathered that it wasn't her husband the man wanted but a servant, a cook, who had apparently once worked at the house. She had never heard the name and did not know how long Hassan had been with Robert and Joanna, but she listened to the man's long and complicated story and then, trying to be helpful, she asked him once more to sit down and wait for her husband who might have heard of the cook. The Arab thanked her but declined to wait. He walked off down the road and she returned to the house and her book. She thought nothing of it.

It was when she took her tea cup through to the kitchen to rinse it that she noticed a window leading to the small back courtyard was wide open and the catch broken. The dust below was marked with the print of sandals. Someone had come in that way. It looked as if someone had climbed out again too but she couldn't be sure and, in case the intruder was still in the house, she telephoned the police station and her husband. Hassan turned up five minutes later and became very frightened. However, she had persuaded him not to run away and he had compromised by mounting guard on the veranda where he was sitting when we arrived.

Pauline told us all this quite calmly and I took it on myself to go through to the bedroom. I didn't think there was anybody still there but the break-in seemed too quick for a robbery and I wondered if the man had left a booby trap behind. We'd had one good man blown to pieces and I didn't want it to happen to another. I looked out for a trip wire. (Never cut a tight wire or pull a loose one, that's what they said.) There were no wires. Everything looked exactly as usual. The house was really a bungalow, a spacious line of interconnecting rooms. To get to the main bedroom where Robert and Joanna had slept you had to pass through two smaller rooms and then through the big bathroom. All the rooms except the bathroom also opened onto the veranda. It was a house I loved but now I wished it didn't have quite so many doors to open because if a door is booby-trapped with a home-made bomb there is no foolproof way of coping with it. All you can do is stand well back so that you are sheltered by the wall and put out your arm to open the door. The explosive will be clipped either behind or above and if you are careful it won't kill you. But it may blow off your arm.

I took the torch in one hand and opened all the doors like that with great care and nothing happened. When I got to the main bedroom where the shutters were closed and the light was dim and green I shone the torch into the light bulb in case that had been replaced with a bomb. That was all right too. Perhaps I was wrong. Perhaps they had taken something after all.

'What's missing?' I asked Pauline.

She looked round and noticed at once. 'My ring. My little opal ring was on the bedside table.' You could see it upset her. 'It belonged to my mother,' she said, 'when she was a girl and she gave it to me. It wasn't worth anything much.'

No, nothing except love. Her handbag was lying on the bed. I was surprised they hadn't taken that too.

'Look in your bag,' I told her. I was sure they would have taken her keys with a view to coming back at some more propitious time, but no, her keys were still there. The purse was gone but she said there had only been a few piastres in it, less than a pound sterling.

'What the heck are they up to?' I asked.

Batty went over to the dressing table to make sure his gold cufflinks were safe. I heard him exclaim and swear and then, as he pulled out one drawer after another, I saw why.

All the clothes had been ransacked. We opened the wardrobe and it was the same. Everything had been handled and left higgledy-piggledy. I sat down on the bed and heaved a sigh of relief. It was all perfectly simple once you knew how. They hadn't come to leave a bomb. The ring and the purse were a cover so that it would look like a simple burglary. What someone had done during the afternoon, while I was safely out of town and they thought the two Battys would be at the tennis courts, was search the house. They had searched all the living rooms and it wasn't till they got round to the bedroom side that they realised Pauline was at home and that they couldn't finish the job. They had retreated and their own ingenuity had got the better of them. They had played the simple trick on her and while one man kept her talking on the other side of the garden another had got into the bedroom to complete their work. Well done, boys. What I wanted to know was what they had been looking for.

'I want you to look everywhere,' I said, 'not just in here, and tell me if anything's missing.'

They were vague about their possessions and didn't seem quite sure what they had left in England and what they had brought out to El Aasima. Sometimes a book could have been missing or it could have been lent to friends. We drank a lot of beer as usual and I made them go on looking and in the end Batty straightened up and said that nothing was gone and he was fed up with the whole thing and it was time we went along and found out why the police hadn't turned up to examine the footprints and get the whole thing properly recorded.

Pauline smiled at me as if she was afraid of making a fool of herself. I'd been such an idiot over the bombs that I told her not to bother about that and to tell me what was worrying her.

'I'm knitting baby clothes,' she confessed. 'I know it's early, but it's a sort of therapy. It calms me. I like it.'

'Well?'

'Since lunchtime, my knitting pattern's gone. I left it on the desk. It wasn't a proper knitting pattern. It was published in the *Observer* and I typed it out. I put it under that ashtray so it wouldn't blow away in the breeze from the cooler, and now it's gone.'

She sat down in one of the yellow chairs and looked up at us. 'I don't know why anyone should take a knitting pattern. However,' she added, her perplexity vanishing, 'it doesn't matter because I think I kept the original cutting. I knew I would lose it sooner or later.

'It doesn't matter,' she said again to reassure me. She smiled her gentle smile and I smiled back. I couldn't understand the theft either until she hunted for the cutting and put it in my hands, a flimsy strip of airmail newsprint like chalky tissue paper. Then I saw.

Mrs Batty had typed out a lacy pattern which was mostly abbreviations and lots of figures. Mrs Stuart had typed out figures, too, but hers were statistics, details of soil conservation and technical data on crop yields. Perhaps the two sets of figures would look much alike to an illiterate Arab. No, for this job they would have sent a man who could read. But he would have needed time to get to grips with our Roman script. Perhaps he hadn't been sure about the knitting pattern, particularly as it must have looked rather like the documents he was searching for.

I had stumbled on the key to the mystery. Mrs Stuart's missing research papers had not been stolen by the Arabs. They were still looking for them. They knew that I had come to pack up Duncan's personal possessions, so they thought that I was looking for the papers too. That was why they were following me around and distracting me. They reckoned that I would find the papers and try to take them home with me. They had briefed my two young followers to intercept me, then seize the briefcase from my hand and get away.

It was as simple as ABC. Only I didn't know where the papers were any more than they did, or the Battys did. I didn't even know that the missing papers were important or secret. Were they anything more than the groundwork for a Ph.D. in Rural Economics? Perhaps they were. Perhaps the fact that the author had been murdered and the papers themselves were missing meant that I was in something I didn't understand, right up to my neck.

I felt much happier now I knew they were not after my blood. We left Hassan still mounting guard on the house, but I didn't think anyone would be giving him any trouble. They would be expecting us to return any moment with the police. I wondered whether it was worth our going to the police but they like to be notified and the insurance people prefer it that way. So we all set off to the area police station across the railway lines.

The police station was a low white building with a dusty green roof. Inside it was dusty too. We sat on school-room chairs and I acted as interpreter while Pauline explained to an inspector. Of course she could not describe the man who had come to the gate. No, she could not even say how dark he had been. The slow flush on her face and neck betrayed her English susceptibility. She shifted uneasily in her chair and it occurred to me that she had no particular desire to have the man caught and confined in the hot, insanitary jail. Only she had considered the consequences of actually arresting one of our burglars. She made me wonder what I wanted out of this business. Justice, yes; but did that mean punishment or rehabilitation? To her it meant stripping a man of his robes and turban and separating him from his wife and children. She wanted no part of it.

The police officer went on writing. Outside it was growing dark. How many times Duncan must have sat here reporting the burglaries on his house. Nothing is ever solved.

A constable came in with a report to make. There was a quick Arabic interchange before he went off duty. I watched him plod down the road, his legs as dusty brown as his khaki uniform puttees. A policeman gets ten pounds a month, his uniform and the statutory house for himself and his family on a police estate. It is less than Hassan earns as a cook with our company, less than any domestic servant in El Aasima. How much can you expect from such a man when it comes to protecting our superfluous property? It is all heavily insured anyway.

The Inspector smiled at me because my Arabic was good. Arabs often exclaim with delight at the purity with which I speak their language. Of course it is pure. It is a language Robert taught me out of books, and is utterly false. No one in El Aasima has spoken classical Arabic for centuries. But the Inspector was an intellectual and he would have liked to. He agreed to bring one of his best trackers down to the house.

It was too late, of course. With skill one could track the intruder across the courtyard, over the wall and a little way along the street outside. Then all trace was lost. He had disappeared more than an hour before between the clay walls of the houses. Somewhere in another kitchen where the servants were brewing coffee and making their ritual sunset prayers, Pauline's ring was being passed from hand to hand. We would never see it again.

The policeman, as usual when there is no other lead, picked on the servant.

'Are you sure of your servant?' he asked Peter. 'It must be your cook.'

Poor, loyal Hassan. He made no protest but stood listening in desperation to the flow of bitter Arabic. The Inspector insisted on taking Hassan back to the station for questioning. We forbade it and in the end, because we were white and Hassan was our servant, we got our way.

I walked back to the Land-Rover with the policeman because I was tempted to tell the whole story. I wanted to know what this man had done when Duncan was burgled and also what he had done when Duncan was killed. But I did not know him well enough to ask and so I let slip the opportunity. In the final analysis I am a coward and do not wish either to kill or to be killed. Nor had I any interest at all in the missing research papers, however valuable. My loyalty, like the policeman's, is to my organisation and the interests of its shareholders.

Duncan's affairs were now wound up and his belongings packed. I was going back to London. Tomorrow before I left I would pay a courtesy call on the British Consul and tell him my story. He could, if he chose, take the matter up with the authorities. It is the Consul, not I, who registers deaths and represents the interests of British citizens who become enmeshed in Arab law. Duncan's problems were not my problems and I was going home to take my leave. I would have liked to take Joanna to the Norfolk Broads and teach her and Robert how to sail . . . the children could wear new yellow life-jackets. They would love it.

Batty brought me a drink and Pauline disappeared to ask Hassan about the supper. He was too shaken to produce anything much, but I accepted their hospitality. I stayed to eat with the Battys because I felt faintly anxious about them. I wondered if the people who were chasing me would start to chase him after I had gone. That was the snag. Would they follow Mrs Batty who was pregnant and ought not to be upset?

I couldn't stay in El Aasima and look after them. In the hurry of leaving London I'd had to come in on a Tourist's Visa which was only valid for a month. Mohi el Din would hardly want to fix me up with something better. I was about to explain to Peter when the telephone rang. It was Carole. Mohammed, her servant, had had his keys stolen in the suq. Someone had used them to get into her flat and steal an antique rosary and her camera.

I am no fool. I had already removed the film from her camera. It was in my pocket and I intended to give it to the Consul in the morning. Carole was indignant about her camera. Although I had paid her for the film (handing over the dirty pink banknotes into her white hand as we stood on the pavement outside the office in full view of passers by), I had assured her that no one would touch the camera now it was empty.

I had to go with her to the police station and sit through the procedure all over again. Only this time it was Carole sitting beside me telling the Inspector what had happened. I loved the sound of her Southern English voice and her unruffled cheerfulness. I loved the way she moved her head as she talked. In fact I wondered whether I wasn't beginning to love Carole in earnest. She asked nothing of me, that was the trouble. She had travelled such unaccountable distances from the small, conventional village where her parents lived outside Bournemouth. As we came out of the Inspector's office and stood in the darkness by the dusty drainage ditch in front of the police station, she slipped her pale hand into mine, and I held it, accepting what she offered.

Chapter Eight

THE BRITISH EMBASSY STOOD in a big square in the centre of town. When the rains came the square sprang green overnight. At other times it was a dusty expanse of nothing at all which served only for military parades (with bands like you find in mining villages in Northern England) and for demonstrations. It was a bad place for demonstrations but the Embassy was agreeable. I love British embassies abroad. One was supposed to go along there and sign a book when one arrived in El Aasima so that if there was any trouble they knew whom they had got on their hands to evacuate. I had forgotten to do this but the Consul whose name was Ralph Pigeon knew that I was in town. Batty had told him when registering the deaths.

Next morning I put on a tie and made myself look respectable. Then I drove the short distance from my hotel to the Embassy. One of the reasons I like embassies is the way they demand this sort of respectability. Another is their assertion, even in the entrance hall, that only the British know how to behave rationally in this unpredictable world. I knew even before I entered his office that Ralph Pigeon would receive me with courtesy and would listen attentively to everything I had to say. He turned out to be a comfortable-looking, middle-aged man with smooth dark hair and a lot of coloured pencils on his desk. It felt like going to confession. I took off my jacket as he invited me to and sat down in a Ministry of Works chair with my feet planted firmly on a green English carpet. Then, feeling very much at home, I broke the news that Duncan had been murdered. I opened my briefcase and put the thin buff file onto his desk so that he could see for himself what the police had had to say. He read the papers slowly and carefully while I sat and watched him.

'You are not satisfied?' he asked at last.

I shook my head. I told him about the hub caps and the life insurance and all the other evidence which pointed to violence.

'Yes,' he agreed, 'I think I would go along with you. The Stuarts must have been threatened with death. But that in itself is not evidence that they actually died a violent death. It could have been an accident.'

I told him how I had been followed, and handed over the film with the pictures of the men, asking him to send it home by diplomatic bag and get it developed where it couldn't be tampered with. I told him about the previous day's robberies and about Mrs Stuart's missing papers.

He pooh-poohed a little and said her research had not been secret. Everyone knew about it. It had been connected with some vast project at the University and he was sure I was wrong about a hunt for the papers. That was only conjecture.

He brought me back to earth with a bump. I began to look at the world in a calm, English way again. At once I saw that it probably had been a road accident which killed the Stuarts.

'What about these burglaries and my being followed?'

'Well, I should certainly go to the police and make a statement about that. I'll get the film developed for you and we'll see if the pictures help. But aren't you due to leave?' he asked.

'Yes,' I said. 'But I'm worried about my staff. I don't know whether I can leave them at such a moment.'

'There's not much one can do about this type of burglary. Our people get burgled, too, you know. We employ gaffirs. A dog or a gaffir seems to put them off. Oh, London won't authorise it, of course. We have to pay for gaffirs out of our own pockets. I have a dog. He's a fat old Sealyham I bought in Beirut years ago. He wouldn't hurt a fly but he barks a lot and that does the trick. I don't know what your people in London are like. With us it's a question of taxpayers' money.' He sighed and then turned to the notes he had made and began underlining very neatly in different colours. I was glad to see my nightmare about murder reduced to the substance of bureaucracy.

I crossed to the window. 'If you're satisfied, I might as well go back to London. I'm supposed to be on leave.'

Far below I could see the two Arabs with the Embassy drivers who waited all morning with their cars parked under the trees.

'There they are,' I said. 'Come and take a look for yourself.'

He came and together we stood peering down. Two little boys were washing down the taxi.

'Why don't you show them to the police?'

'They never follow me to a police station. I showed them to one of my friends in the Ministry of Petroleum.'

'What did he say?'

'He didn't know them. Or so he said.'

'But he could have sent them packing?'

'Depends who they are, doesn't it?'

'I'll get rid of them for you. I'll ask our police sentry to identify them.'

'That would be kind of you,' I said.

Those men murdered Duncan, I thought, and if they didn't they know who did. But I didn't say anything because I knew Pigeon didn't believe me. I dreaded to think what it would do to my career if word got back to London that I was making wild accusations about murder.

So Pigeon and I talked about the general welfare of our people and the role of the Consulate, if any, and the coffee came and we sipped it out of the tiny cups and drank the icy water that came with it. Eventually Pigeon said what he had been gathering courage to say for the past quarter of an hour.

'Of course,' he said in a casual way, 'if it did turn out to be a murder, then we should have to take a very serious view of it indeed. It would be of quite considerable importance.'

'Of course,' I agreed. 'It would really pose quite difficult problems for us too.'

'The effect on the British community here might . . . the people out here are easily alarmed.'

'What are you going to do?' I asked him sourly. 'Wait and see if another of our men gets bumped off?'

He was annoyed with me for saying that but I felt angry too and didn't care. 'No, forget it,' I told him. 'I'll fly home towards the end of this week and leave you in peace. But I feel it has been useful our having a chat.'

He nodded. 'We're pleased to see you any time, Mr Patterson. I hope you have a good flight back.'

I left for the office and the men didn't follow me. Later in the morning Mohi el Din rang up to say he had been onto the police and told them to warn the men off. Was I still being followed? I had to say no and he took the credit for it. I felt out of temper with all the world. It was as if Pigeon and I had had a friendly game of tennis together and I had lost when I ought to have won. 'A useful chat' had I said to him? Not useful enough . . . yet, had I known it, it was that cautious, kid-gloved circle of diplomats who were going to blow the whole thing up.

In the meantime I took every action I could to prevent it. I had Ali brought in from Duncan's house and asked him to find us some good guards as a temporary measure and someone said that the English wife of the manager of the tobacco factory knew all about guard dogs and bred them. I left Batty to deal with that because a commissioner of police from Headquarters arrived to see me. He had come to apologise both for the burglaries and for my being followed. He apologised as if it had been his own fault which

I was sure it wasn't; I had always got on well with the police. However, I guessed that Mohi el Din was behind the visitation so I took it very well. I used the opportunity to explain that Duncan had not just been robbed but had been threatened as well. It was a good thing, I said, that the police were certain he had died in an accident and had witnesses to prove it, because otherwise our people might be very alarmed. If anything happened to Mr Batty or his wife (who was pregnant, I pointed out), then we might have to reconsider the whole question of expansion. It wasn't worth while making surveys if we couldn't work the oil wells in peace.

I was carrying on in this way and congratulating myself on the flow of my Arabic when there was a knock on the door and it flew open to reveal Carole looking harassed. Behind her there stood a large man I had failed to remember over the years. I would have liked to have met him in the desert, this Fahd I had heard so much about. I would have liked to have taken a Land-Rover and driven out to the camp where he was working and to have walked across the sand to shake hands with him unannounced. I would have done that if I had had time, but I had not and now he had me at a disadvantage. He was sweaty and dusty from the drive into town. I was the Englishman, clean and cool and superior, sitting as I was at Duncan's imposing desk. He grasped my hand and turned at once to greet the Commissioner with the traditional Arab courtesies and blessings I love to hear. How did they come to know each other I wondered. Did they know each other closely or had they met at one of Duncan's cocktail parties for people who mattered?

I sent out for coffee and asked Carole to bring cigarettes. One gets out of the habit of these things but Duncan would have expected it of me and it gave me a chance to take in the two men. There was quite a contrast. On one side sat the policeman in his Western-style uniform and with his peaked cap on the desk before him. He wore a lanyard, a shining belt with holsters, and all the accoutrements of official authority. Fahd wore a bedouin head-dress twisted roughly round his head without the benefit of any fancy cords to hold it in place, but with it he wore a shirt and trousers which made him look like a navvy, which he wasn't. He was a big man and his movements were forceful. Even in the office, he behaved as if he were out in the desert. The Commissioner moved and talked with the grace of the old Arabs, which looks effeminate to Western eyes.

Fahd had inherited none of these affectations. He was our fault. He could have been an American. I think he would have talked to me in American English if I had let him but I had been speaking in Arabic when he came in and I went on that way because I wanted him to give me a chance, just as I was prepared to give him a chance. I didn't ask him to like me but I hoped for his respect.

At last the officer took his leave and Fahd and I called in Batty so that the three of us could discuss the company situation and how work was progressing. I get twinges of conscience when I think I am neglecting the company. Our real business is to get the oil out. Humouring everyone is only a means to this end. Fahd knew about getting oil out and I hoped he would tell me a bit about it. But he was as deferential towards Batty as Batty was towards me and volunteered nothing unless actually asked for his opinion.

Carole sat in the corner making notes but it wasn't a useful conversation. I was bored with Batty and Fahd seemed difficult. Eventually I gave up and called a halt, suggesting that we meet again in the evening. What was needed, of course, was Duncan, who could have handled both men. Duncan had seemed cold and impersonal but he would have run that meeting without a hitch. At the end he would have outlined business for the next month and left it at that. He knew about decision-making. Finally he would have stood up and handed the files back to Carole with a smile. Would he or would he not have invited Fahd out to lunch? I didn't know. That was the trouble. We used Fahd but we didn't know him.

Carole waited in the doorway as we dispersed our various ways. I had nothing to say to her. I had no excuses for leaving her and no reason for staying. I told her to book me a seat on the first available BOAC flight to London, then changed my mind and asked her to make it Rome because it would be nice to have a couple of days in Rome, fare paid, on my way home. She didn't seem much affected. She had known I would have to go. She smiled at me and made a note on the green pad. I picked up my unwanted jacket and went downstairs alone, intending to walk to the hotel. It is hot in the middle of the day but inside a car it can be hotter still. I felt like walking.

Fahd was on foot too. He must have brought his Land-Rover into El Aasima for repairs and now he was walking down to the taxi rank by the Embassy. I ran to catch him up and then didn't know why I had stopped him. I had nothing to say. Fahd didn't mind. Like all Arabs he had an inexhaustible flow of courtesy.

Suddenly he said to me in English, 'It's a pity you can't come back with me and have a look at how things are going. It would interest you, I think.'

'Yes it would,' I said. I thought about it and then I said, 'I might do it yet. If there's no place on a plane till next week, I've finished here. There's nothing more for me to do here. It's all in the hands of the police.'

'I was expecting you all week,' he said. 'I thought you'd want to check up.'

'No one needs to check up on you,' I said.

He came back to the hotel with me then and I asked him to wait while I went to see if there was any mail. There had been a flight in from London the night before and I hoped there might be something from Joanna. There was and I was pleased. I came back grinning and as we sat down to have lime juice he begged me to go ahead and read my wife's letter. He knew what it was like to be separated from his family and to have to wait for the post. I put the letter on the table. 'No, I'm not married now. It's not from my family, just an old friend I always stay with in England. Her husband worked in the company here for a time. You may have known him, Robert Prentice.'

He reached out for the letter. It was a flimsy blue airletter form with Joanna's neat italic handwriting across it. Her own name and address had been filled in in the proper place on the back.

'Yes, Joanna,' he said as if making sure of something.

'So you remember them?'

'As if it were yesterday.'

The waiter came with the tall glasses of crushed lime. I put in a big spoonful of sugar and stirred it round among the ice cubes. There is a nice ritual to drinking limoun, a satisfying clink of ice against glass. I was thinking of Robert.

'A waste of a good man,' I said. 'One occasion on which Duncan boobed.'

'Mr Stuart did not "boob'," Fahd said, and he inserted the English slang into his Arabic with great distaste. He picked up a peanut and ate it and then he said, 'Robert made the mistake of despising office politics. He thought he could be above them. He was not friends with Mr Stuart and he ought to have been.'

I took my cue from this. 'But Robert was one of your friends?'

'Yes.'

'He is one of mine, too.' We set traps for ourselves round the world by clinging to what is over and gone. I pulled out my wallet and extracted the little snapshot of Joanna and Robert with their children. 'There,' I said, 'you see it has all blown over and they are doing very well. They are happy in England.'

'I would not have thought so,' he said. 'This country was very important to them.'

'Yes it was,' I agreed. 'They remember it incessantly. They're homesick, if you like. If Robert didn't have so many Arab students back in England, I think he would have to come out to El Aasima to teach, simply for the pleasure of having Arab friends and speaking Arabic.'

'Yes, he is a good friend of the Arabs.'

'And yet, it's funny, everyone here has forgotten him completely. You're the first person I have met who remembers him at all.'

'I don't think he has been forgotten,' said Fahd. 'Perhaps they don't like to admit it.'

'And you do?'

'Yes,' he said. He got out his own wallet and showed me a bundle of photographs fixed together with a rubber band. They were mostly of his own family: a plump, smiling Arab woman and two little daughters.

'My friends laugh at me because I have no sons,' he said as he showed me the pictures one by one. The last picture showed him with Joanna and her children in England. 'Robert took that,' he said. They were in the garden at the front of Robert's house and the children looked younger than now. Judy still had her baby curls. It was two years old perhaps. 'I was on a management course in London,' he explained. He searched a bit further among his lists and notebooks and found an old airletter in Joanna's writing. It was the twin of mine. He put it on the table as one plays a trump card and we both laughed.

'It's a good thing we have met,' he said. 'I'd like you to come to my house and meet my wife. It is she who keeps in touch with Joanna.' I was surprised he had a wife who came out socially.

'It's an eccentricity of mine to have an emancipated wife,' he explained. 'Selima is a midwife. Joanna was a great friend of hers. My wife was the first girl from this town to go to England alone to finish her training as a midwife. She was in Manchester but by now she has forgotten most of her English. My wife delivered Robert's first child. A son,' he added proudly. 'She would like to meet you.'

I knew I would have to go to his home to meet his wife.

She might be emancipated in his eyes but she would certainly never come out to a public place like a hotel, particularly one where they still sold alcohol.

'Is your wife expecting you for lunch now?' I asked.

'Yes.'

'Then you must go. I don't suppose you'll be staying long in town?'

'Depends when the truck is ready. I thought I'd go back this evening or tomorrow morning. I only came in to speak to Peter Batty about getting some more men on the job.'

'Casual labour, you mean?'

He nodded.

I didn't say anything because he hadn't asked my opinion. My opinion of Arab casual labour was in fact low. Men came to us badly fed, exhausted from sleeping out while they looked for work, and sometimes suffering from TB and bilharzia into the bargain. The company prefers us to keep our own men, give them a regular wage and health checks, and get a good day's work out of them. It's not hard to find labour. There's not enough work to go round and that's where we come right up against the old-established Arab way of managing the problem. In El Aasima there is no unemployment as such. They have underemployment. Batty strives to employ on a full-time basis and to pay well. The government would rather we paid less and took on more men.

Fahd said, 'The American Aid Programme road through the cotton mills has ground to a halt. They've got five kilometres through Bahra and the government can't decide to go on. No work's been done there for ten days now and the men have been laid off and are drifting back to their families. If I send word over to Bahra they'll come to us. They're used to road work. I really could do with them and some of them I could put onto building culverts. The American road is going to be held up three months; I had that estimate from the guy in charge who comes to us for his whisky. I'd arrange with him to release his men back to him when he's ready to get on with the job.'

'What did Batty say?'

'He said he'd have to telex London.'

'Will the answer come in time?'

He shrugged. 'Buchara,' he said. 'Mr Batty always asks London.'

'Take the men on while you've got the chance,' I said.

'That's what I'm doing.' He was a practical man.

'And if London veto it?'

'They won't.'

I wondered why he was so sure.

'After Robert left, Mr Stuart usually took my word for things,' he explained. So London were used to rubber-stamping Fahd's decisions were they? I thought back to the files I had examined in the new tower block high above St Paul's. I saw he was right.

'So Robert's leaving here was a good thing for you?'

He shook his hand at me crossly. 'Robert gave me my job. Robert and I did things together for years. But I'm more diplomatic than Robert. I had to get on with Mr Stuart and now I have to get on with Mr Batty.'

And with me, I thought bitterly. 'I'll come with you if you can wait in town till tomorrow,' I said.

I saw he was pleased. It gave him a night with his wife which he might not have allowed himself and it gave him my company for a couple of days. 'By the way,' I said, 'have you heard this rumour that Duncan Stuart and his family were murdered? That there was no accident?'

I could see it from his face that he had heard. There was sweat on his forehead and behind his ears. He was going to dismiss the story as market-place gossip and then he thought better of it and just nodded and said, 'Yes.'

'What's your opinion?' I asked him.

'It's possible.'

'Is there anything we can do about it?'

'No, nothing.' He drank some lemonade. 'There have always been rumours,' he said by way of explanation.

'I know,' I said, because I did know. Men sat drinking cardamom coffee in the cafés round the suq and stories flew like wildfire round the town and died and sprang up again and became common knowledge.

'I've been scared,' I said. 'There have been two youths following me.'

'But that's all over. They were students with a grudge.'

'Against me?'

'Against Mr Stuart.'

I sat up at that but he laughed at me. 'Not to kill him or any of us. Maybe they're boys who have gone through university with a view to getting a comfortable job with us . . . with an oil company or in the Civil Service or one of the banks. They haven't a lot of choice. Then when it comes to the point they fail their exams or don't get that position they hoped for, which would give them a car and a western-style office and all the electrical goods a European has, and they feel let down. So what next? They've got no work, so they follow you around, hoping your car will break down and they can do you a service. Then out of gratitude you may get them a job. That sort of thing happens to me all the time,' he said.

I didn't disbelieve him. It was a plausible story but after he had left for home I sat in a dark corner of the hotel bar and decided that he was lying. It was a pity because I wanted to like Fahd.

I wished I had Carole with me to take my mind off it. I wished I could take her into the desert with me. Though I knew it was impossible, I longed to have her beside me in the truck and to smell, through the dust, the scent of lilies of the valley which she wore for her open-air life of tennis and swimming at the club. Fahd wouldn't mind my taking a girl. Fahd would smile and turn a blind eye. Batty would believe I needed her along to take dictation. But there was an over-riding reason why she couldn't come. The engineers and mechanics we had out there at the drillings, men without women, would find it tough if I turned up with a bird in tow. I put my job before my pleasure because, when it boils down to it, that's the way I am running my life. The job comes first. With Robert it doesn't. He has Joanna.

Chapter Nine

FAHD AND I SPENT the first night in Bahra where the walls of the Government Rest House are as thick as my arm. At ten the generator was switched off and the fans on the ceiling above us came to a slow stop. We slept quietly, wrapped in the half-warm, half-cool air of the old house. It was a reservoir of shade. Next morning we were up at four when the heat of the sun was not yet a hardship and the light was as soft as it ever is in the desert. After Bahra we headed into the distance where there was nothing but sand and rock and an oil field.

Fahd said little. We had called a truce, neither trusting the other. We were driving along part of the road Fahd had built, alongside the pipeline. We call it a road out there but all he had done was to lay gravel on the soft sand patches and make the wadis passable by building culverts of concrete. Like any desert road it wore into ruts and corrugations. Fahd had an American grader which he put over it two or three times a year to smooth off the surface.

'What d'you think?' he asked.

It was a great improvement.

'I like it,' I shouted back.

I like the desert. Even when I started out in hydro-carbons and worked out there in the desert on surveys for months at a stretch, with only the occasional binge in a washed-out town like Bahra, full of children and flies, I liked it. Fahd was on home territory, too. With the Land-Rover we caught up with his gang of men working in the inevitable dust. They were stripped to vests and loincloths or shorts. They worked slowly, doggedly, in the great heat, and Fahd got down and walked up and down talking to them, shouting above the noise of the bulldozer. I'd have liked to see him use more trucks and machines out there, but manpower is what came first and was what had built that road. Once the road had been firmed up with gravel and a bit of proper drainage I hoped we wouldn't have so many vehicles getting stuck between Bahra and the well head.

At the road camp Fahd had an old army tent as a temporary office. The men slept in blankets in the open. There was water in an old oilcan for washing. It was better than nothing. Sometimes there is no water for washing at all. That night I wrote up my notes by the light of an oil lamp when I ought to have been asleep. It was very quiet. I could hear, muted with night, the laughter of some of the men who had made coffee on a biscuit-tin stove and were now sitting round the glow of the charcoal they had used. Fahd came and fetched me out of the tent to sit with him.

'It's going well,' I said.

He nodded.

Far above us the Southern Cross hung at the extreme of the starry sky. I never felt out there in the desert with him that there might be bombs planted or plots laid, but he brought it all back to me by saying suddenly:

'You remember what I was saying the other morning about Robert, and the need for diplomacy?'

I nodded.

'It's a tip,' he said modestly, 'just a tip but you might bear it in mind.' He paused to light a cigarette. 'You asked me about Duncan Stuart. You think I've not done my job. I've not asked questions or tried to find out what happened.'

'No,' I said.

'That's how I saw my job,' he said. 'I kept quiet, Mark, because the company's interest seemed to me to depend on that sort of tact. What you do is up to you.'

I said nothing. I wondered what there was to say.

'Do you understand?' he asked anxiously. He was concerned that I shouldn't think he had fallen down on the job.

'It's too late,' I said, 'I've already been to the British Embassy about it.'

'Ya ahkee, I would not have done that,' he despaired with a shake of his head.

'They didn't believe me any more than you do,' I added.

'Then they'll do nothing,' said Fahd.

'Besides, it's not dangerous,' I told him, 'I've a good friend at the Ministry, Mohi el Din Saad.'

Fahd shrugged. I wouldn't have expected him to like Mohi el Din. Politically speaking they were poles apart and jealous as cats of each other's influence.

'I hope,' said Fahd, 'that it will all blow over.'

'At least we don't have to worry about it out here.'

We lay on the ground and I scratched patterns in the sand as we talked. One by one the lamps went out and the men slept like shadows in the moonlight round their charcoal stoves.

Fahd said, 'You're happy.'

'I wish this were my country,' I said.

He nodded. 'I like it too. But I grew up in a town. My father was a schoolmaster. I used to envy the boys who were real bedou and belonged out here with their camels and goats.'

I nodded. It was a vanishing world.

Fahd said, 'If I weren't so busy I'd like to read books about the desert. There's an Englishman who comes into our main camp from time to time. He plays chess with me. He says that here in the desert there are several hundred different types of plants and flowers. He says that the old tribesmen knew them all and how to make use of each of them for food, or pasture or medicines.'

'I doubt if they use anything like one hundred nowadays,' I said.

'But the plants are still here. He knows them.' It seemed to me that such knowledge was a luxury.

'It must take a lifetime,' I said.

'Yes. He told me he first heard of them from a gunner he met one night when he was in the British Army in the Sahara.'

It was a strange train of events I thought from those two soldiers sprawled against their tank to us resting by the road in all that peaceful wilderness.

'He was badly wounded in the fighting near El Adem,' said Fahd. 'He told me he never met the guy again.'

'Do you know everyone in the desert?' I asked.

'Most of them,' he said.

He looked across at the shape of the Land-Rover with the long metal sand tracks strapped to the side. 'We'll go on to the camp in the morning. You can sleep in an air-conditioned caravan tomorrow night if you want.' I didn't want to. A patch of ground between the thorn bushes was enough for any man.

I said, 'I've got to go home, Fahd. I can't stay.'

'Tread softly, my brother,' he said, and that was all.

I got back to town much later than I had expected. I had planned to spend the last evening with Carole and then ask her to drive me out to the airport to catch my plane. If I took her out to dinner at the Italian restaurant where they serve European food and have waiters in white coats like in London, then I thought she wouldn't mind.

I was feeling happy when the driver dropped me off at her block. In a way which Carole (showering three times a day, glistening with soap) would not understand, I like to get dirtier and dirtier. My shirt had darkened and looked old. My arms and face were ingrained with the yellow-brown stain of sweat and sand. I was as stained and worn as a cowboy. I somehow hoped the glamour of it all might excuse me for not having washed and changed my clothes. But I was in a hurry to see her.

She opened the door and looked at me as if she were seeing a ghost.

Her voice, her words, betrayed nothing. 'I've had to change your flight booking three times,' she said. 'BOAC are fed up with you . . . and with me,' she added.

'Good girl,' I said.

She kissed me, gave an enormous sigh, and to my horror said, 'We thought you might be dead.'

'What nonsense. I was enjoying it so I decided to stay. Fahd said he would ask someone to telephone from the depot that I was staying out at the rig with him.'

Since she had kissed me, I bent and kissed her. She brushed the tears out of her eyes and grinned. 'They are all hysterical here,' she told me by way of explanation.

'Why? What's been going on? More burglaries?'

'No. The Ambassador called on Mr Batty.'

Good grief, I thought. No ambassador had ever called on me. 'What did he want?' I asked her.

'I don't know what he wanted,' she shrugged. 'I'm not supposed to know what he wanted.'

'You tell me all the same,' I said.

'It was about the Stuarts being murdered.'

'But they weren't murdered,' I said. My mouth went dry.

'The Ambassador suspects they were, or might have been. He's got the whole Embassy working on it.'

'What did poor old Peter do when he heard that?'

'He said what you said, that Duncan Stuart wasn't murdered.' I still had my hands on Carole's shoulders. I moved them gently up her skin and onto her shining hair. I was thinking. I wondered whether the Embassy had got any new evidence. The betting was that they hadn't, that it was simply Lady Silcox who had been disturbed by what I had told her about Janet, and had confided in her husband. And her husband, out of a very British sense of loyalty to Duncan, had remarked casually, as ambassadors do, that it might be worth looking into the circumstances in which Duncan Stuart had been killed.

When ambassadors make casual remarks like that, their staff take action. Ralph Pigeon would have come bustling in with his fastidiously arranged papers and they would have held meetings and written more minutes. No wonder Batty was hysterical.

I laughed. I think I was pleased with myself for bringing up the big guns like this, however unintentionally. Now we would get to the bottom of the mystery. I was only sorry that I wouldn't be around to unravel it myself. My Tourist's Visa was about to expire. Batty on his own would be running round like a cat with nine kittens. I suspected that the Police Department might be beginning to run in circles too, not to speak of the Ministry of Petroleum. It depended how much dust the Embassy had kicked up.

She said, 'Everyone has been ringing you up. London, the Embassy, the police, the Ministry. They all want you urgently.'

My heart sank because I knew they would get me as soon as I stepped out of her door, and once they had me bunched up with people of importance there would be no more Carole for me that night. Maybe not any night if the eye of the town was upon me. I settled my arms closer about her.

'They can wait,' I whispered as much to myself as to her. She smiled. She was not a girl for giggles. Her cropped head dropped onto my dirty shirt. It was bliss to be back. It felt like a honeymoon and I think we enjoyed it more.

Afterwards, lying on her bed with my shoes off, I reached for my wallet and pulled out Joanna's airletter which had got a bit crumpled on its journeyings. I had read it a good few times.

'Listen,' I said to Carole, 'I want to read you part of a letter. Just lie there and listen.' She was sleepy and her face was beautiful when she was sleepy. The eyes were large.

Joanna wrote about the children and Robert. She said

she was making a big effort this year to teach the children to swim and that her grandfather was very ill and that they had had a puncture coming back from their holiday. When it came to Janet Stuart she said,

> In answer to your question: No, I didn't know Janet because she didn't let me. She was a snob . . . intellectual and otherwise. She patronised me when we met, like someone from a class above us (which she may have been). She made it clear that she was bored by Robert and me, which is ironic now Robert is a Head of Department here and a proper academic because *her* sole claim to distinction was as an academic. She used to carry on a lot about women's equality and how important it was to keep on with one's own work . . . which I hadn't, so she had no time for me.
>
> She was immensely proud of her sons. I think she liked Duncan less, but either way it was a restrained, well-bred love. She had no idea how I could be happy just playing with the baby, nor how frantically I sometimes felt for him and for Robert. I read some things she wrote from the University Library. Very dull and lots of jargon I didn't understand though I dare say her fellow academics did. So I can't judge her academically. Sorry not to help you more but I hardly knew her except as the wife of Robert's boss who used to entertain us to dinner and cocktails purely out of a sense of duty because it was part of her job. She did it grudgingly, that's all I can say. But I expect she was more interested in her research so she has my sympathy. I would have liked to have known her but it was her fault.

I stopped reading and lay looking up at the grey mesh of the air conditioner. 'How does that strike you?' I asked. 'Does it strike you as reasonable?'

'Yes. I didn't know about the research; did you?'

'Yes. I found out.'

'It is true that she was very gracious to us all. I didn't think she was grudging but she may have been and that was how it showed. She wasn't my type either.'

'The tragedy is that I think she may have been Joanna's,' I said, for Joanna had complained so often that there were no intelligent women in the town. I could picture Joanna putting her baby into the car and driving across the old Arab city to visit Selima because there was no Englishwoman whose company Joanna cared to seek. If Janet had been more relaxed, she and Joanna might have got on very well, and where the wives led, their husbands might have been dragged, however unwillingly, behind. If Robert and Duncan had been friends, the crisis between them need never have come. It was too late now. But I was glad that Joanna had been fair to Janet. Joanna was the first person I had come across who had actually bothered to read what Janet wrote. That was funny. Joanna had done her best.

And what about Carole? Carole lay dreaming, curled against my arm. There was no weight to her. I could have held her a long time. I wondered if I was going to marry Carole simply because she was there and because there was no other way of keeping her. If I did not marry her, I would lose her. We would each be posted our different ways. It's easy in our way of life to say goodbye.

'I must go,' I said reluctantly and sat up. Obediently she sat up too and all that was left of our love was the widening patch of damp upon the sheet where the sweat had run from us like water. Love in the tropics is not fastidious. Her hair had lost its red and turned dark with the sweat which had trickled down behind her ears. Even when we separated we smelled of each other. When I stepped through the door she was fresh and newly laundered. I had spoiled all that and left her with my sweat on her white skin. She had been touched by the desert. I had been dirty to start with but now she had mingled herself with the sand and I knew from the feel of my skin and the hint of lilies of the valley that I had come from her bed. I buttoned my shirt and picked up my bag. I was not even sure that she would marry me if I asked.

I walked to the hotel. All the violent tennis and swimming that goes on among my colleagues is a frantic attempt to keep fit in a climate where it is not seemly for Europeans to walk. I have no time for a sporting life and am content to go on foot. So it was that I walked into the modern concrete lobby of the hotel. The sudden air conditioning was horrible. The souvenir stalls were horrible. I hated being back in El Aasima. Two journalists, one English, one German, were over at the bar. I could tell from the way they put down their drinks when I came in that they had been waiting for me. If the press were on to this story it must really have blown up big.

It was the man I hadn't noticed who caught me, though. There was suddenly a hand on my arm and I swung round to find Mohi el Din smiling his charming smile. Softly, politely, he greeted me by name. He had been sitting waiting in a black plastic armchair just inside the doors and I hadn't recognised him because I was used to seeing him in European dress and tonight he was all the Arab. He was spotless, his skin bathed and scented, his robes all brilliant white from the wash. They were fine robes, robes fitting for the successful son of a wealthy family. His jallabiyah was intricately stitched in white, his flowing cloak was held by a gold chain with ornaments. He had gold rings on his fingers and the white folds of his fine headcloth were layered one on the other, exactly in place. He was beautiful.

He shook my hand and asked after my trip and my health and my plans for the future.

'I'm flying home tonight,' I explained. While I am still in one piece and can make the most of my leave, I thought. But to him I expressed infinite regrets at leaving his country and my Arab friends so soon.

His smile was very winning. You could not guess from his smile that he must have waited every evening for a week, watching for me to return so that he could catch me. He invited me to go back with him and join some friends from the Ministry who insisted on entertaining me before I left. It was never possible to refuse him when he asked in that way with his brilliant, hopeful smile. I didn't even want to refuse because Arab ways have their charm for me and in any case it was politic to fall in with the suggestions of the Ministry, parties and all. In their published diaries Englishmen exaggerate the horrors of Arab food. I like it. I am probably greedy but whether it is couscous on the Mediterranean, burgul to the East, beans or chick peas, sour pancakes or the unleavened bread of the desert: I can eat it all.

'I'd be delighted to come. It's really most kind of you. But you must excuse me for keeping you waiting a few minutes longer. First I must wash and change my clothes.' I indicated with disgust the stains on my shirt and trousers. Then I grabbed the key of my room and made for the stairs. His hand was still on my arm and I had an all too certain suspicion he was going to come with me. He didn't want to let me out of his sight. But I had on clothes in which it was possible to run up stairs. Mohi el Din did not. So I ran for it. Once in my room I locked the door and telephoned Batty. He was so thankful to hear me that I regretted not ringing him from Carole's. He poured out his worry and distress. He had never believed in the murder story, he still didn't, but he was the sort of Englishman abroad who found it difficult if not impossible to have a difference of opinion with his ambassador.

'Of course,' he said hopefully, 'this means you will be staying on.'

'I don't see why I should. I have every confidence in your ability to handle this.'

It wasn't true. But I wanted my leave and I kidded myself that I was doing him a good turn. The very fact that London had sent me out in the first place showed how little they relied on Batty. If he could manage on his own now he would do himself the world of good. Any ambitious man would have jumped at the chance.

Batty had a gift for doing as he was told. He could be relied on for that. He also knew how to get answers from a computer. He had a good degree in economics, an intricate but impersonal subject which suited him down to the ground. With Fahd in the desert making judgements by instinct and Batty in the office making the judgements of science, Duncan had done very well for himself. If you asked Batty a question he would go away and work hard and come back with the right answer. No, he was no fool. It was just that he was flustered by people and the airs and graces they gave themselves. Batty could do *The Times* crossword as quickly as anyone I know. On one memorable occasion he won the *New Statesman* competition but he so hated people discovering that he read the *New Statesman* that he gave it up instantly. Or maybe that was just a funny story about him.

Pity moved me. 'I'll stay,' I said, 'don't worry, I'll stay as long as you want me.'

'You must speak to the Ambassador,' he insisted.

'O.K.,' I said. 'But not tonight.' At eight o'clock at night an ambassador is preparing to go out to dinner. He would not be pleased to hear from me.

The murder of our manager, however earthshaking to us, was not going to feature all that big on the agenda of an ambassador. Yes, his life might be boring in that tranquil Arab outpost but he would have routine business enough to keep him occupied and over the years he would have achieved a sense of balance. Ambassadors do not work themselves up into a tizzy. Nor was I going to.

'I am dining with Mohi el Din and some friends. You might ring BOAC for me and cancel the flight. I'll be in in the morning and if anyone from the Embassy rings, you can tell them that I'm grateful to them for looking after our interests so carefully and will be calling on them at eleven o'clock to discuss progress.

'I want you to come to this dinner with me tonight,' I

said. 'You must leave Pauline, take her round to Carole's flat if she is scared to be left alone. Then come on to the hotel and ring me from the reception desk. I'll wait in my room till you arrive. You'll find Mohi el Din in the hall and also two journalists. Don't talk to them. The journalists I mean.'

Obliging as ever (he was almost as obliging as Carole), he agreed at once. I didn't tell him that I had been scared of going to the Arab party alone. I had never been scared before.

I sat on the edge of the hotel bed and decided what to wear. When I am with Arabs whose robes are like Persil advertisements I feel shabby in my suit. It has sweat stains round the collar and the pocket sags because I have overloaded it with my wallet and my pens. I stripped off and had a shower. The hotel shower worked for once. I shaved and rubbed aftershave into my skin. It smelled terrible and stung on the sunburn. Then I put on a white polo-necked shirt and a white cotton suit I had bought in Amsterdam where clothes do not always obey the rules. I wanted to meet my Arab hosts on an equal footing now. As a last flourish I put on my sunglasses. They are Zeiss glasses with brown tinted lenses meant for the glare of the desert, not for social occasions after dark, but they made me every bit as inscrutable as Mohi el Din. The only snag was that in those fancy white clothes there was no pocket or recess in which I could conceal a gun.

The gun wasn't mine. It had been Duncan's and I had taken it from among his things. In fact it was so small and light that I suspected it had been Janet's and that his had been on him when he died. Like Joanna, I had done a course in shooting and Fahd and I had practised together out in the desert. So I wasn't too rusty. I thought I would be able to hit a man if he wasn't too far away. That was about all. I wasn't one of those shots who could hit a hand or a leg at will. Reluctantly I decided that a gun would be inappropriate that night. At any rate I hoped so.

When Batty arrived puffing and sweating he stared and he hummed and he hawed but it wasn't till we were walking along the passage on our way downstairs that he plucked up courage to say, 'Far be it from me to criticise, Mark, but do you think London would like you to go to an official party in that get-up?'

'I'm expressing my personality,' I said.

He laughed, unsure of himself and of me.

'That's what our hosts are doing tonight.'

I arranged with Batty that as a precaution he and I would go in his car, following Mohi el Din. I was glad of that because a group of three resplendent Arabs awaited us in the lobby, a strong escort.

We drove in convoy through the darkening town. The air was yellow with dust. Along the river by the University where it should have been better, Batty complained that the sand was stinging his eyes. He kept blinking as he drove. I took off my dark glasses, opened the door of the car as we went along and sniffed. It felt like smoke in my eyes too.

'Tear gas,' I said. There were traces of tear gas, too faint to smell, too faint to make one weep. Tear gas six or seven hours old, that's what it smelled like to me.

'Have there been demonstrations while I've been away?' I asked him.

'I've read nothing about it in the papers, though yesterday one of the lads in Accounts said there was going to be a protest. Against the government of course.'

'Why this time?'

'The government is being too soft on the occupied territories, apparently.'

'Anti-Israel demonstrations.'

'Mmm.'

'Then this is the the aftermath. If there has been nothing in the press, that means the authorities must be trying to hush it up. They've held the students back here by the college and not let them get as far as the centre of town.'

'Are you afraid? . . . For the future I mean.'

'If the government are jittery then I suppose we ought to be. If there's a nationalist coup then I guess that's the end for us. We get nationalised.'

'And they lose a lot of their royalties . . . '

'It's the principle of the thing,' I reminded him.

Chapter Ten

WE WERE DRIVING THROUGH my favourite part of the town and there were trees along the road and in the gardens. It's an in-between area. It isn't the old Arab town and it isn't the modern suburbs where Americans and successful Arabs live. The houses we were driving past had been put up between the wars or in the forties and early fifties. Some of them had been built by Armenians or Greeks and Italians and had a nice southern European flavour. Others were Arab and had managed to retain some traditional Arab qualities, thick walls and courtyards where there was shade.

We stopped at a big house. It was not one I recognised but I guessed from the way Mohi el Din talked that it belonged to his father or maybe to his uncle. These big family mansions house several generations, but I had been to Mohi el Din's home and I knew he did not live here. This was altogether grander with a big walled forecourt where there were plenty of people around. None of them took any notice as we walked through; they just went on with what they were doing, talking, bringing coffee, mending the rope mesh of a wooden angareeb. The presence of all these men showed the importance of the owner of the house. They were his family retainers or distant relatives who had drifted in from the desert and were now enjoying his hospitality. They had come to look for work or to buy and sell at the suqs or perhaps they had come for a family wedding. They had come to ask a favour or to enjoy one. Confined to the outer courtyard they were subservient without being servile. It was where they belonged. They were tied by the family tie.

We walked quickly between the squatting Arabs and in at the door of the house, into its rooms which is where we belong. Inside, the walls were covered with family photographs and there were armchairs and sofas in a suite which could have been ordered from Cairo. They were as new as on the day they had been uncrated and were still displayed in the clear plastic covers in which they had been sold. Without this protection the dust would have ruined them long ago. But it is hell to sit on the shiny plastic. In that heat it gets glued to one's legs.

I tried to signal to Batty that I wanted to know where we were. Could this house possibly belong to a member of the government or an Arab ambassador whom I ought to recognise? Had someone important asked to see me and was that why Mohi el Din had been so anxious to produce me on time? We waited for a few minutes among the dark ornaments and plastic covers until our presence was announced. I don't think Batty had been out to Arab houses much for he looked cowed by it all. I wished we could give him a gin to brighten him up, but I knew there would be no alcohol for either of us that night. A few of my Arab friends do drink in the homes of Europeans but in this sort of old-style household there was no privacy. Everything that came in and out must pass through the courtyard where day after day the men would turn towards Mecca and pray at the hours of prayer. My host could not offend their susceptibilities by using alcohol. Funny how I assumed that he would want to drink, that his traditional religion no longer bound him.

'Whose house is this?' I asked Mohi el Din.

'Sayed Abdullah el Nasri,' he hissed.

I had it: he was a successful building contractor, cousin to someone who was always in and of the government, though I couldn't remember his name at that moment, and uncle by marriage to Mohi el Din. Had Duncan known Abdullah,

I wondered. I'd been through the files and couldn't remember Duncan giving him one of our contracts. Perhaps Fahd hadn't trusted him. But Duncan could have known him socially. It was just this sort of Arab Duncan used to like. They might have gone hunting together on a Sunday morning. Falcons and guns and a Land-Rover or two.

We were led up a narrow stairway, then up another and through a small roof-top room out on to the roof itself. Fine rugs had been laid and wooden chairs had been set all round the edge of the roof against the low wall. It looked as if something was going to happen in the middle, but I knew nothing was. That was the way they always set out chairs for a party, one big circle which was already almost complete. Our host, robed like Mohi el Din but with a cloak of dark blue, stepped forward to greet us and summoned a servant with drinks (brilliant syrups like those which French children love but adults taste with suspicion). We talked for the required minute or two and I was led to a chair.

Looking round quickly I saw few faces I recognised. In spite of what Mohi el Din had said about this being a party thrown for me by the Ministry, it was obviously nothing of the sort. It was Abdullah's party to which he had invited his family and his business connections among the old Arab élite. Apart from Batty and myself there were no Europeans present and I doubted whether any would arrive after us. As I had foreseen, none of the guests were in European dress; all were in spectacular robes and wearing a fortune in golden jewellery.

I recognised three faces only (others I remembered from long ago but could not place). When I was younger I moved in less exalted circles. I recognised a retired member of the provincial government service who was an expert on land law and was now a judge, I had met him at Mohi el Din's house once before; the Assistant Chief of Police whose face I recognised from press photographs; and a young half-brother to Mohi el Din who was still doing his medical training (in Rome, I think). I knew him and we talked together. Darkness fell and the lights were turned on. Half an hour later (had they been summoned by telephone?) a team arrived from the Ministry of Petroleum Affairs. They were led by Mohammed Ismael, the Under Secretary to whom I had spoken on first arriving in El Aasima.

Thank God that the days were long past when I failed to recognise my business contacts once they had shed their Italian business suits. It is a psychological sleight of hand, this transformation wrought by flowing robes. During office hours I work with these men. We are oil men together. We transcend nationality. But that night they had separated themselves from me. First and foremost they were Arabs and they greeted me as if I were their guest (as indeed I was) in their country, in their milieu. We sat and we talked for an hour or two. There is no shortage of time during these evenings. It is the custom to talk until late at night and only then will a meal be offered. After the meal it is courteous to take one's leave at once. So we talked and, though I tried to find out what was going on in town (tear gas? demonstrations?), they denied these things and I gave up asking.

After the desert nights, the atmosphere of the town was heavy, suffocating. Still we talked and the stars showed palely over the glow of the city. I was introduced to many influential men. All seemed anxious to talk to me but none was willing to talk to me about anything connected with the oil business or the government, the things which interested me. Usually such an evening would depend largely on political gossip and I was disappointed. I did not seem to find my feet and spent my time paying compliments for want of anything better to do. I hoped to goodness Batty was having the sense to do the same.

I was feeling hungry and there was no sign yet of any food. I put my empty glass down on top of the wall and walked out of the circle of chairs to a place where I could be alone for a moment or two. In the street below a tethered donkey brayed and was quiet again. I could smell the dust in the air. At last someone moved up behind me as I had known someone would, someone who wanted to speak to me. I turned and it was the Police Chief leaning on the parapet beside me, enjoying the view of the night sky through the eucalyptus trees.

'A pleasant evening,' he said.

I thought it was nothing after the brilliant moon and stars which arch above the desert at night but I didn't say so. I nodded and went on leaning on the balustrade. Sooner or later he would get to the point.

'You have been away?' he asked, and I told him about my visit to our men at the oil field.

'In your absence,' he went on, 'your friends from the British Embassy have been in touch with us. The Ministry of Foreign Affairs is handling the matter for them. There is great concern . . . '

'Yes, I am concerned,' I said.

'It is a happy thing that we have met tonight,' he said, 'because I believe that everything can be explained. Indeed, it's better that it should be. The rumours that are flying round the town are quite unnecessary and will do great harm between our countries. If you were worried you should have come direct to me.'

'I found it difficult to trouble you over my personal feelings.'

'Yesterday they were your personal feelings perhaps. Today even your ambassador is asking us questions . . . At your request,' he added accusingly.

'I am sure your assurances will satisfy the Ambassador,' I said politely.

'Mr Patterson,' he said. 'The affair is delicate.'

I took that to mean that he hadn't been able to give the necessary assurances. Somewhere, somehow, the Ambassador (who employed the best local legal advisers and knew how to needle his way in Arab affairs) had caught the Police Department out on some detail or another.

My heart beat faster. So they had covered up for someone. Duncan had been murdered. I was almost glad. It was quite irrational to be glad about a murder but I suppose I was glad because I had been right and all my caution which had seemed so eccentric really had made sense. Maybe the time had come for me to remove my own hub caps.

'We will all of us be only too glad to co-operate in your investigations,' I said.

'Further investigations will not be necessary,' he answered. 'I am satisfied. The case has been closed by my department.'

'But you have made no arrest.'

'I feel that it would not be politic to proceed.'

'Why the hell not? He was murdered in cold blood, wasn't he?'

'I didn't say that.'

'But you believe it. You have reasons for believing it.' His face was expressionless. 'Will you listen to my reasons, Mr Patterson? I think they would interest you. You should also explain them to your office in London because this could have been a most serious matter for all of us.'

'I am sure it could be,' I agreed. 'Go on.'

'We have good evidence that your manager, Mr Duncan Stuart, was an agent for the Zionists.'

'Duncan Stuart spying for Israel?'

'If you prefer to put it like that, yes, Mr Patterson, we are absolutely sure.'

'Can you prove it?' I asked, knowing he couldn't, for no one, no one in creation, was less likely to be an Israeli spy than our dour Duncan. He wasn't even an Israeli sympathiser. (English anti-semitism was ingrained in him more like a habit than a vice.)

'If we had completed the case against Mr Stuart then he would have been arrested and charged. We would not have allowed him to continue his work. As it was, he was warned many months ago that it would be better for him to leave this country. He did not go and this is the result which he brought upon himself.'

'I suppose he denied the charge?'

'He did, yes.'

'Because,' I said angrily, 'it's all nonsense. He wasn't a spy. No one would believe that.'

'What else can we believe, Mr Patterson? Here is a man who spends all his free time photographing our country. He makes records of every place of interest and his wife at the same time investigates even the smallest of our villages. Nothing escapes them, and all this information is freely passed into the hands of our country's enemies. This is unheard-of provocation, Mr Patterson. The deaths did not surprise me one bit. A known friend of the Zionists has no friends here and many enemies.'

'I'm sure,' I said. God, I was thinking. God, what can I do? No oil company can afford to have its manager unmasked as an Israeli agent. If this became public knowledge, we would never get them to accept anyone from London ever again. There was Fahd, of course, but I didn't think he could manage everything single-handed. And the Arabs hadn't got the technicians anyway. Without European experts the whole thing would disintegrate. And I was on difficult ground with my denials because I was in a country where it is not the truth that matters but what people wish to believe. It would be embarrassing to have nationalist demonstrations against the government so, as far as they are concerned, there were no demonstrations today. They won't admit that Duncan was one of the truest friends the Arabs ever had and so, as far as they are concerned, he was an arch enemy. So truth disappears because it is denied. Duncan is transformed into a tool of the Imperialists, a fully fledged spy with camera and codes. Because they prefer him that way.

Yet it didn't make sense. How could they prefer it? How could a government admit to its populace that it had negotiated vital oil leases with a Zionist? How could they risk these same students who had marched about at midday, turning on our offices next time and jeopardising the oil revenues? The answer was that they couldn't and this was why I had been brought to the strange house, to meet a man out of uniform and do a deal with him. I would no longer press for an inquiry into the deaths and he would see no one knew of the Israeli aspect of the story. That seemed all right to me, provided of course that Duncan had been an agent. No one had yet offered any evidence that he was.

'Naturally we have been watching Mr Stuart for some time, as soon as we were led to suspect these illegal activities.'

'And did you discover anything?'

'It was not difficult,' he said simply, and from the folds of his jallabiyah he took an envelope which he handed to me.

'Go on,' he said, daring me, 'open it.'

I opened it and pulled out two photostats. The first was of a pamphlet with photographs, describing the progress of various charitable enterprises in Israel: a children's home, a farm school and so on. The second, which was actually addressed to Duncan, was a circular letter. His name had been filled in by hand. His address in El Aasima was typed at the head of the letter. In the photostat I could not tell whether the signature at the end was a real one or a facsimile. I will not embarrass the organisation concerned by giving its real name. It is a perfectly innocent charitable foundation and would give no offence to anyone but an Arab. When I unfolded the letter on that faraway roof top, the name at the head of the notepaper meant nothing to me. Why should it have done? Occasionally I contribute to Oxfam or the Salvation Army. I had never had anything to connect me to Israel. That night though I could guess what I had come across. EYTAN FOUNDATION it said in English lettering and alongside was some Hebrew lettering which presumably gave the same name in Hebrew. There was an address in London and one in Jerusalem.

It read

Dear Mr Stuart,

We have appreciated your support of our work in the past and it is for this reason that we are sending you this account of our year's activities. You will see that with the help of our many friends, including yourself, we have achieved our plans to help in the creation of the new kibbutz of B—— in Hebron. However, our young people who have set out to make a new life for themselves there still lack much of the modern equipment without which no worthwhile agricultural development can go forward and become self-supporting. Our target for this year is the purchase of further high-capacity water pumps. They will provide the essential irrigation that will enable us to double the area at present under cultivation with all that that means for our young and growing community. I feel sure that you will . . .

I didn't read any further. I didn't need to. This didn't prove Duncan was a spy but it was bad enough. Not a nice letter for Duncan to get through the post. I couldn't imagine anything more damaging in Arab eyes. No, not a nice letter to get . . . But had he received it? I wondered.

'Have you the original?' I asked.

'We have, yes. It was intercepted in the post.'

'So you had already had word from somewhere that Mr Stuart might be up to something?'

'We have our sources of information, yes.'

My immediate reaction to the letter was that it was a hoax. I didn't even know if the Eytan Foundation was a genuine organisation. I thought it could be some spiteful Arab plan to discredit Duncan and have him sent packing.

'Is the letter genuine?' I asked. 'Have you checked on that?'

'Our embassy in London tells us that this organisation is listed in your telephone directory. It is a known centre of Zionism.' Obviously he had expected me to know that. I felt awkwardly that he was waiting for me to apologise for not knowing everything about Israel and its offshoots.

'This is a duplicated letter,' I pointed out. 'It doesn't actually prove that Mr Stuart contributed a penny to this organisation, or that he was ever in touch with it. They could have mailed this to him in error.'

'I do not think my Department is wrong,' he said solidly.

'Have you any other documentation?'

'What else could we need, Mr Patterson?'

I was on shaky ground myself now. If I seemed to think that the letter in my hand was not incriminating to Duncan, I would immediately incriminate myself.

'Take it home, read it carefully and destroy it,' said the Assistant Chief of Police. 'I for my part will see that the original is also destroyed. No one will hear of this matter from us and we rely on you to keep silent, also. There is no need for anyone else at all, not even your embassy, to know the inside of this matter. For the sake of our future business, Mr Patterson (and I know you are a true friend to us Arabs) I think we should let this case rest now. Let it, as you say, die a natural death.'

There was no point in arguing. Duncan hadn't been a friend of mine and I wasn't prepared to jeopardise the company's future in El Aasima just for the sake of unravelling his death. In any case, even supposing I tracked down his killers, it was now clear that they were members of some pan-Arab nationalist group and that the Police Department was not in a position to arrest or to jail them. Duncan was dead, dead, dead, and in my hand, thrusting into my trousers pocket, I hid away his paltry, insignificant death warrant.

'All right,' I said. 'I will do exactly as you say. I'm sure it is for the best, and perhaps I should say how grateful I am to you for your handling of this affair. How truly sorry I am that the good name of our company has been used in this way.'

He did not lead me in to eat. It was the young doctor who took my arm and motioned me into the adjoining room where a buffet supper was now laid out. There were tiny roast chickens, dishes of stuffed vine leaves, savoury stuffed pastries and little succulent cutlets of lamb. I was shaken but still hungry and was not sorry when my hosts piled my plate over-generously and I was begged to eat. Suddenly everyone seemed to have relaxed. It was clear that the business of the evening was over and now we could begin to enjoy ourselves. I did my best.

Next day it was my formal suit again. I went to call on the Ambassador. I thanked him for his concern and told him how helpful he had been. I said that I was sure that it was his intervention and that of his admirable staff which had prompted the Police Department to let me see other reports which substantiated the rather sketchy account of the accident which was all anyone had seen up till then. I said that I myself had spoken to witnesses and as a result I was now returning to London completely satisfied that Duncan had indeed been responsible for his own death. I said how reassuring it was to be able to go back and report to our people in London that the Embassy had spared absolutely no effort to get at the truth of the matter, and how much we appreciated his own interest and concern and that of his gallant team.

We parted friends and everyone seemed as pleased with themselves as the Arabs had the night before.

After I had washed my hands of all that I wandered down the suq to get presents for the folk back home. I bought nuts and beans and fresh dates for Robert and Joanna because I knew they would like them. For the children I went to a tailor's shop and bought miniature jallabiyas for dressing up. Joanna is always saying that they love dressing up. These white shifts are dirt cheap in the shops along the suq because they are what the poorer children wear. Rich boys wear shorts and shirts nowadays and look rather French in them. For Judy I bought another carved wooden camel at the hotel souvenir stall. Silly really. They are produced in their thousands throughout the Middle East, but I rather like camels and so does she.

I packed and I sat in the hotel and thought about leaving

Carole. In the end I sent her some flowers which in El Aasima is like giving a girl pearls or orchids. Flowers in the English sense don't exist in the desert. Only a few are flown in for the rich and reckless to buy from an air-conditioned flower shop near the main square. I had never been there before but I thought she deserved to be a millionaire's mistress just for one day.

I took a case of Duncan's private papers to the BOAC freight office so it could fly back with me. The police probably went through it with a toothcomb before letting it out but in the end they cleared it, probably because Janet Stuart's research papers had still not been found. Not by me at any rate.

Then I left. It was as simple as that, simple as it always is for a European to escape from the heat and the dust. Far below, like the country of a myth, you watch the blue sea and the Greek islands, then the coast of Italy, golden with sun, then you cross the Alps and it is over and you are back in the northern wind and drizzle where you belong.

Chapter Eleven

LIKE AN ASTRONAUT RETURNED from the moon I was going to have to be debriefed. There was no chance of getting away from London for a week or two, so I did as Joanna was always pressing me to do. I went straight to Robert's house and settled in with them. I hated the idea of going back to stay in my club.

I had a good time with the Prentices but that has nothing to do with the story, my story which I first hinted at over the telephone to Michaelson. He was about to leave with his family for a holiday on Dartmoor and he wasn't pleased when I turned up with a case full of complications. He called a conference and we met in his office which felt very cold to me. They never have the central heating in these places turned on in summer and it is pretty chilly when you've just got back from the desert.

I showed them the photostat of the letter from the Eytan Foundation which I had not destroyed but had simply put in my pocket and brought home with me. There were several possibilities, none of which we could prove or disprove. The simplest was to give the Arabs the benefit of the doubt and agree that Duncan and his wife had been doing some sort of information work for Israel and had been killed in the course of their duties. How ridiculous we were, middle-aged English businessmen sitting round Michaelson's office and trying to make up our minds whether another middle-aged English businessman like ourselves had hoodwinked us all and had really been something quite different.

Michaelson thought he had been. He said that taking the photography and the research work into account the Arab case looked pretty strong.

I said that no self-respecting spy would have broken his cover by contributing to an Israeli charity.

Michaelson said that that had been an error, just a clerical error in the charity mailing office which had thus broken the cover.

But I remembered that the cover had been broken already. I had been told that the police only started opening Duncan's mail after someone had tipped them off about the spying.

Michaelson thought he could explain everything by saying that the Arabs had been tipped off by one of their own agents, or by a double agent who knew the Israeli organisation, but they had had no luck at all in pinning anything definite on the Stuarts. They had therefore helped themselves along a little by arranging to have this letter sent. The letter would have been enough to make us understand why they wanted Duncan withdrawn and replaced.

I didn't see much future in the drawn-out discussion. Duncan was dead. If his murderers were, as I suspected, a militant group of nationalists then the government wasn't in a position to make any arrests. Too much was at stake. So, like it or not, the case was closed. No one from the company was going to go back out there with a gun and do a bit of shooting to even things up.

'So let's forget Duncan,' I said, 'and see what we ought to do to stop this happening again.'

Michaelson took this to mean security clearing of all our chaps to make sure they weren't really intelligence agents in disguise. The thought of our personnel department handling this was enough to make anyone laugh. Company men just don't carry on that way . . . people like Duncan and Michaelson and me. Why do we join Super Oil? Because we are people who are used to doing well for ourselves, used to coming top in exams and shining at interviews? Because we are people who are sure of ourselves and of our company with its convenient blue-chip status on the stock markets of the western world? Not for us the doubts and moral scruples of American youth, the ivory tower of campus and college. We are practical men at work among the realities of life.

On a different plane altogether Arab may fight Israeli, but these are other men's quarrels in which we play no part. I have no views on anything but the interests of the oil business and if these involve my tacit commitment to the Arab, well that's a company decision taken on economic grounds (the computers churn out estimates for profit and loss). We are men without political emotions. We do not become spies. Duncan had been one of us. I could not believe that he had sacrificed company interests (his own interests) for those of a small Jewish state perched precariously on the edge of the Mediterranean and offering minimal rewards.

I cleared my throat as if to speak and they all turned to listen. I said, 'I have spent the last month going through the Stuarts' things. Now I feel that I know the man, the kind of man he was. I do not believe he was engaged in intelligence work of any kind. I believe he was killed in a quarrel which did not concern him, in fact I will hazard a guess that this is a case not of espionage but of blackmail. I reached for my briefcase and pulled out a sheaf of notes I had typed up at Joanna's. I know how these things ought to be done and there was a copy for everyone.

'This is my evidence that Duncan Stuart was being threatened over a period of months. I would like us to consider why he never mentioned it to any of us.'

They all sat up at that because I was insinuating that it might indirectly be their responsibility, this tragedy they did not quite understand.

'On the one hand,' I said, 'we had Duncan; educated, intelligent and with apologies to you, Isaacs,' I smiled at the fatherly man on my left, 'mildly anti-semitic.' Isaacs went pink. 'One day someone sent Duncan a letter saying that he was suspected of pro-Israeli sympathies. Later he was accused of making substantial contributions to the Eytan Foundation, a charity of which he had never even heard. One by one the restrictions hit him: his camera permit was withdrawn, his wife was refused permission to visit outlying villages to complete fieldwork vital for her research. He was advised to leave the country. He did not. He did not even write back to Personnel Department and ask Isaacs here to transfer him. Instead he stayed on. He was not a coward. He wanted to complete the re-negotiation of the leases because he believed that he could handle it better than anyone else, so he did not mention the threats even to Michaelson who was his area co-ordinator. His life was threatened. He could have telexed you, Mr King, in Welfare Department. But he didn't. He stayed on and was killed.'

'Why?' I asked Isaacs. 'Why?'

'Who knows why? Suppose he had written to London in the beginning and said that the Arabs were giving him hell because he was supposed to have contributed to some damn Israeli charity. What would your reaction have been? To you, to any of us, that would not have been a crime. The stupidity would have been letting the Arabs find out about it. Besides, supposing this slander, let us call it that without prejudice, supposing this slander had been passed round the Arab camp from capital to capital, he would never have been granted a work permit in any Arab oil-producing state ever again. He would have had no future. If we'd known we would have been dead scared at what was going on and how it would harm our reputation among the Arabs. We couldn't have handled it. Duncan knew that. He knew we'd throw him out whatever the truth of the matter. We couldn't use him abroad any more and he wouldn't have been much use to us here in London, you know what these old-school expatriates are like . . . so we'd retire him early and there'd be a golden handshake and he would be out in the cold world, fifty years old and suddenly nobody, nobody any more.'

'Poor devil,' said Isaacs.

Mr King said, 'This is ridiculous. He should have asked us. That's what we're here for.'

'What could you have done?' I asked. 'You could have saved him from the Arabs, but could you have saved him inside the company? The company can't afford to keep dead wood.'

There was silence while we all meditated on our own uncertain futures in the company and the prospect of being pensioned off at fifty as dead wood.

'Somehow, some way,' said Isaacs after a bit, 'we've got to persuade our people to turn to us if they get into this sort of trouble. The question is, how?'

'That's your problem,' I said quietly. 'That's what I wanted to say. Please don't let it happen again. I can tell you from experience that it isn't very nice being sent out to clear up afterwards.'

'The interesting thing,' said Michaelson, an area co-ordinator who really took an interest in his area, 'is whether the same thing will happen to our next man out there . . .'

I looked round at their faces. None of them was senior enough to have much say in the appointment of Duncan's successor but I thought it worth trying. 'In my opinion,' I said, 'our next manager out there ought to be an Arab.'

Michaelson said, 'I suppose that was just what they hoped we would think. That's why they murdered the Stuarts. Bastards.'

'We can't let them get away with that,' said King.

'Let who?' I asked. 'The man I have in mind had nothing to do with the murder. He had nothing to gain from it and since he was Duncan's right-hand man he risks losing out, I suppose. His name is Fahd Mohammed Ahmed. He knows everything about our business out there and is probably capable of running the whole show.'

'It has never been done before,' said Michaelson.

'I know,' I said. 'I just hoped you and Isaacs might mention Fahd if anyone happened to ask you what I thought.'

'I will,' said Isaacs, 'but it won't make any difference.' All the same Isaacs unscrewed the top of his fountain pen and made a note of the name. I was surprised that he wrote it in Arabic as Fahd himself would have written it. Many of us learn to speak Arabic but few of us learn to write it. Isaacs took a pleasure in forming the letters. I enjoyed watching him do it.

I hung around in Surrey for a day or two but no one called me and finally Michaelson said I'd better take my leave. I did. I hired a car and went to Yorkshire, to the dales and the moors. Sometimes I slept in hotels, sometimes I camped. No one disturbed me because no one knew where to find me. Then I got tired of being by myself so I flew to Amsterdam and spent a long time looking at some of the greatest pictures in the world. I have friends in The Hague and we sailed together. It was nice. I like Holland and I was sad to leave. I sent Carole a postcard of a windmill.

When I got back to Joanna's the summer was over and there were all sorts of letters and messages, including an urgent one from Michaelson that he wanted to see me. Joanna said he had used all sorts of choice language over the phone when he learned that I had gone off without leaving an address. We're not supposed to do that but I'd already had my leave spoiled once and wasn't going to risk it happening again. Michaelson was anxious because I had been summoned to appear before the top management. What now, I thought, what now? They'd all been pleased with what I'd done about Duncan and I was greedy for a good job.

I was apprehensive when we walked in that door, because the company is apt to send bachelors to vile places where dangerous things happen and life is generally less comfortable. The manager took off his glasses, laid them carefully on his blotter (I didn't know people used blotters any more) and said firmly that it had been decided that as I'd done so well in the interim, I was probably the best person to succeed Duncan Stuart in El Aasima. It was obviously going to be rather a sensitive job for the next few years.

I had to be unsentimental about it. That was good news for me. It was promotion about six or seven years before I would even have started hoping for it. I was going to get a lot more pay and I was going to be in charge of a show of my own. I was surprised really and I think they both saw I was surprised because they began to reassure me that they had thought about it carefully and believed I could do the job. I knew I could. (Later I was to learn that the Ministry of Petroleum had dropped a hint through their embassy in London that mine would be an acceptable appointment. I suppose they thought they had bought my silence.) I didn't refuse the posting or try to dissuade anyone. One doesn't look a gift horse in the mouth after all. But how strange it was that in the end I was the only person to profit out of Duncan's death.

The manager looked down at some notes on his desk and said, 'I see that you think highly of this fellow, Fahd Mohammed Ahmed?'

'Yes,' I said. 'He's first class.'

'I'd like to meet him' he said. 'Why don't you bring him over for a week or so, then we could discuss things with him.'

'That's an excellent idea. Actually,' I went on, 'he could hardly have more responsibility than he had under Duncan Stuart, but I feel we ought to pay him more.'

'You think we'll lose him to someone else if we don't? Is he that sort of fellow?'

'I am sure the Americans would like him,' I said. I didn't think Fahd would quit the company but I knew that if I said he would stay without the extra money, he'd not get what he deserved. A business is not a charity.

'Yes, of course. And we really depend on this Fahd, do we?'

'We do, yes.'

'I'll endorse your recommendation then,' said the great man. He made another note or two and we left.

Chapter Twelve

JOANNA AND ROBERT WERE delighted about my promotion. They put a bottle of champagne in the fridge (they had been saving it for their wedding anniversary but I got it instead). We had kebabs for supper and then Joanna made pancakes and I turned them into crêpes suzettes, which is about the only thing I'm good for in the kitchen. I said they must come and stay with me in El Aasima for old times' sake and they said of course they would and we talked till after midnight. But later, lying in bed and listening to a cat screaming in the next-door garden, I had more sober thoughts and could not sleep.

A day or two later I took the two children to London for the day to see the guards changing at Buckingham Palace as it says in the poem. Then we walked through St James's Park to see the pelicans. It was a lovely day and the park was full of civil servants picnicking on the grass. I bought some sandwiches too and we had our own picnic and fed the crumbs to the sparrows and pigeons. Afterwards we went for a little walk. I suppose I had known for a long time what I was going to do; it was just that to go up to London specially was somehow too much of a good thing. But that bright afternoon I led the already weary children to a quiet street and found the house. It was a perfect red brick Georgian house with a white front door and the brass plaque on the railings saying 'Eytan Foundation' in English and again in Hebrew. It was a quiet, neat plaque as befitted the road we were in.

I glanced quickly up and down the row of houses to make sure that no one in particular was watching us and then I led the two children up the steps and in at the front door which swung open to my touch. To our left was a white-painted door marked 'Enquiries' so I knocked and went straight in. I thought the sooner it was done the better.

There was a girl in the room and she smiled at me. I could see she was going to be nice. She looked like a nice, polite English girl. Was she Israeli? I didn't know. I am not one of these people who can tell a Jew by his feet. She smiled at the children, who turned suddenly bashful, and I took out my wallet and handed her the creased photostat of the fateful Eytan circular.

'I wonder if you can tell me,' I asked politely, 'whether this is genuine?'

She looked down at it quickly and then up again. 'Yes, this is ours,' she said. 'Why? Did you think it might not be?'

'It was sent to a man working in the Arab world. I thought that maybe you would have some sort of rule about not sending publicity material to Arab addresses.'

'We don't have a rule,' she said. 'I don't think that it would ever arise. We just don't have subscribers who live in Arab countries.'

'Well, you can see for yourself that it happened this time.'

'Yes, I see,' she said gravely.

'Maybe we could have a look at your addressograph,' I suggested. 'Then we might find out how it happened. For instance, is it filed by country?'

'Yes it is . . . but no Arab countries. This one must surely be muddled up with the United Kingdom addresses.'

'Could you check for me, please? You see, I'd like the plate removed and destroyed so it doesn't happen again.'

'Excuse me a moment,' she said. She disappeared somewhere, probably into what had once been the cellar of the house. I sat by the window and watched the empty street and tried to prevent the children touching anything. She came back after a time with an inky plate in her hand.

'I found it,' she said, and showed me. 'I'm sorry,' she said. 'It was silly of us not to think. We won't do it again. I will tell the secretary about it so that from now on we shall have a rule.'

I said, 'That's kind of you. But it puzzles me how this name came onto your mailing list in the first place. Is your list only of people who have contributed?'

'That list, yes. The green tab means he contributed.'

'Can you give me any details?'

'Oh, I don't think I could do that. Donations are supposed to be confidential. No, I couldn't tell you.'

'I'll have to ask to see your boss then, if you can't tell me yourself. You see I have to know.'

She made no objection, took no offence. 'I'll get him,' she said, 'if you don't mind waiting a moment.'

She left the room again and this time she went upstairs. Her boss was a thin, serious-looking man in his early thirties. He looked tired. He was probably not very well paid.

'I'm very sorry,' he said to me as we shook hands, 'but I certainly can't divulge any individual contributions. We don't as a rule do that.'

'I think you might make an exception in this case.'

'Mr Stuart might be extremely displeased.'

'I doubt it,' I said brutally, 'because he is dead. In fact . . .' They both looked shocked and the man interrupted me with his condolences. 'I'm so sorry,' he said. 'I had no idea.'

'He was murdered,' I said. 'He was murdered because you carelessly sent him a copy of your circular letter and the Arabs thought that that was going too far. Hebron is Arab territory.'

The man went red in the face. 'Is this a police enquiry?' he asked. 'Because in that case maybe I could tell you.'

'No, I'm not the police. I'm a friend of Duncan Stuart's and that's why I've come to you for help. You see, I find it difficult to believe he supported you. He was much more likely to be a member of the Society for Anglo-Arab Understanding.'

'In public maybe,' said the man. 'In private perhaps he sympathised with us.'

'Well, he paid for it dearly enough,' I said.

We all suddenly remembered the children and looked at them crossly as if they were to blame for everything. There they were, not understanding, but both staring at us with that fixed look of concentration which Joanna has when she is totally involved with something. With that look she pores over her weekend shopping list or checks the laundry.

The worried man motioned me towards the door. 'Come up to my office,' he said. 'Sarah will keep the children happy. Won't you Sarah?'

She smiled and I knew that she would.

We went up the clean, white-painted stairs and he said anxiously, 'What you ask is difficult, you know. We don't keep records of every individual's donations. All we do is note each day's post, the cheques, postal orders and so on. If you wanted to find out how often and how much your friend contributed, you would have to go through each day's entry over a period of years. It would be searching for a needle in a haystack.'

'I would be willing to do that myself,' I volunteered.

'No, we couldn't open our books to you. It would have to be we who searched.'

I knew it was impossible, that I couldn't ask this careworn man to take on yet another burden.

'It would help me to know whether he paid by cheque,' I said. 'I suppose you don't remember?'

'Sarah opens the mail,' he said.

I wished I hadn't brought the children. It was Sarah I needed to talk to.

'Or could you tell me when he first contributed? Do you date your addressograph plates?'

'I don't think so,' he said. 'Sarah sees to that.' Sarah seemed to see to everything. I wondered what he did in his clean white office upstairs. Was he really working for the

Eytan Foundation or was the young, clean-living Israeli image just a front? Was he recruiting and co-ordinating intelligence agents? Had Duncan been working for him as well as for us?

'The name Duncan Stuart doesn't ring a bell?'

'No, not at all.'

I sat and stared out of his window at the trees. At the back of my mind was the near certainty that when I had been combing through Duncan's papers I hadn't found the name of the Eytan Foundation on any of his cheque stubs.

The Secretary, whose name I still didn't know but who later turned out to be called Spicer, took me seriously. He was desperately anxious to help.

'I suppose there couldn't be a brother or a son, some relative with the same name and initials?' he suggested.

I thought about it. Yes. There had been sons, hadn't there? And it was just possible that one of them (an idealistic undergraduate tempted by the idea of a summer on a kibbutz, a boy in revulsion against his father's uncompromsing Arab view of the world) had contributed. 'Could be,' I said. 'Could be.'

'I am most distressed, Mr Patterson,' he said. 'I feel somehow responsible.' His concern was so genuine, so naive, that I had to take pity on him.

'Well, no,' I said. 'To be fair it looks as though your letter was only part of the picture. The Arabs seem to have been tipped off before your circular was sent. That was why they were on the lookout for it. Who tipped them off or why, I'm not sure. I don't suppose any Arab sympathiser has access to your books. Another suggestion is that they were sure Mr Stuart was working in intelligence for the Israeli government and they needed something to incriminate him. So they made a bogus contribution in his name and then sat back and waited for you to contact him and thus provide them with the evidence.'

'It sounds horrible,' he said. 'I would hate to think we had been party to something like that.'

'You weren't party to it . . . only instrumental,' I pointed out. I got out one of my business visiting cards and wrote Joanna's telephone number and name and address on the back. 'If you do get any ideas,' I said, 'you can contact me here for the next week or so.'

He nodded and put the card away in his pocket. Without speaking (as if we were at Duncan's funeral perhaps) we went downstairs and collected the children from Sarah.

'You've been very good,' I told them and as a reward I took them somewhere smart for tea and bought them big ice creams. Then I took them home to their mother. All the way I was wondering whether I'd carried it off. I'd told Spicer what I wanted to know and I'd heaped the responsibility onto his frail, intellectual shoulders. I had a feeling that before very long he would be getting in touch with me. Maybe I'd even managed to whet his curiosity.

I was right. He rang up at half past nine that night. We were sitting watching television and it was a long time before anyone could rouse themselves to answer the telephone. In the end it was Joanna who went, pulling a face. She came back a moment later. 'It's for you,' she said to me. 'A man called Spicer. Who's he?'

'Thanks,' I said and brushed past her into the hall where the phone was. Spicer was breathless.

'I thought you'd like to know I've found what you wanted.' He must have been going through the books, poor man, ever since I had left him.

'That's terribly good of you,' I said.

'Not at all. I felt that we were indirectly responsible. It was the least I could do. In fact it was easier than I thought. You see, you may be right. These Stuart payments may not have been genuine.'

'Go on,' I said.

'The money was genuine enough, but the provenance may not have been. I looked back until I came across the most recent payment. That was last Christmas . . . as you might expect. Non-Jews usually give at Christmas time and that does for the whole year. It wasn't a cheque, it was a postal order.'

'That's interesting,' I said.

'After that I knew what to look out for. We don't get many contributions by postal order, so I looked for other postal orders and cash contributions and didn't bother with the list of cheques.'

'What did you find?' I asked.

He gave me three dates. 'I don't know how far back you want me to go,' he said wearily.

'It doesn't matter. I wanted to prove something to myself. If he had paid by cheque that would pretty well prove he had made personal contributions . . . but now we'll never know.'

'I would say that he didn't,' said Spicer dryly. 'How could he buy and send us British postal orders?'

'Didn't you think it odd then that he gave a foreign address?'

'He didn't. He doesn't seem to have done. He gave a personal address in Croydon.'

'Yes, that was his home in England. He would have had the Post Office forward his letters from there to our London office.'

'Then your office would have forwarded them on to the Middle East?'

'Yes.'

'I wonder how it is that we came to have a foreign addressograph plate for him then?' Spicer asked.

'I don't know,' I said. 'I suppose you don't file letters asking you to change addresses on your mailing list?'

'No, they're thrown away as soon as they're dealt with. We like to keep our running costs down, you see.'

'Yes,' I said. 'Well, don't you worry about it. I expect their tenants in Croydon received one of your letters at the house by mistake. It must have slipped through the Post Office net and the tenants conscientiously returned it to your office with a note about the correct address in El Aasima. One can see how it might have happened.'

'Yes,' said Spicer.

'I'm most grateful to you,' I said.

'Not at all.' Then he said wearily, 'I'm going off home now. But I'm not happy about it. Are you?'

'No,' I said, 'but thank you all the same.'

'What you said about him being a spy,' said Spicer, thus convincing me of his own innocence, for what intelligence man would ever express himself so crudely over a public telephone line? 'If I hear anything, I'll let you know.' He sounded rather excited about it. I expect he had friends at the Israeli Embassy.

'That's extremely good of you,' I said. I didn't see it would do much harm. The more the merrier, was what I thought. I went back to Robert and Joanna and tried to pick up the threads of the play they were watching. I like watching television. Joanna was calmly knitting with her eyes on the screen.

'What was all that about?' she asked as I settled back in my place.

'A friend of Duncan's,' I said. After that she didn't ask anything else.

The rest of my leave passed quickly. Fahd came and I enjoyed showing him round. Like all Arabs, he was astounded by the fresh greenness of the countryside. We went for walks together on the downs and talked oil. At the end of a week they sent him back to El Aasima with a watercolour painting of St Paul's as a souvenir. I settled to the frustrating task of getting my possessions reshipped and to saying goodbye to my elderly relatives. Then just at the last moment Spicer rang me up again. I had had my final anti-typhoid injection that morning and as usual it had given me a raging fever. It was not a good day to catch me.

'There's a friend of mine would like to meet you,' he said. 'Could you lunch with us?'

'No,' I said blearily. I wasn't risking my neck by meeting any Israelis in a public place.

'In my office then?' he suggested. 'Where you came before.'

'It would be better if you came to my office,' I said hopefully.

He agreed, which probably meant that we were meeting for their benefit rather than for mine. But I kept the appointment all the same and put in my pocket colour prints from a couple of the slides in Carole's camera. They showed quite well the faces of the two men who had followed me so assiduously. I thought I might as well get something out of this meeting too.

Spicer's friend was definitely an Israeli. He was not at home speaking English, but he was polite and workmanlike. I liked him.

'I don't know who you are,' he began, 'but I suppose the fact that we are meeting here in the Super Oil Building does prove at least that you have a respectable profession.'

'My name is Patterson, Mark Patterson, and I am succeeding Mr Stuart as manager of our production company in El Aasima.'

'Not involved in local politics there, Mr Patterson?'

'No,' I said. 'Not at all. Why should I be?'

'No reason. No reason. I just wondered. I didn't like the address you gave Spicer. Thought it might be a trick and you were leading him a little astray.'

'I was perfectly frank with Mr Spicer,' I protested, 'and he was most helpful. What's odd about the address? I'm staying with friends.'

'You know the Prentices well, do you?'

'I've known them for years, yes.'

'Their names are well known to us, too. You must realise that, Mr Patterson.'

'Actually, I don't,' I said. I resent people criticising friends of mine, particularly strangers.

'They are hardly friends of Israel,' he said. 'In fact they miss no opportunity of publicising the Palestinian cause. Hardly a month goes by without one or another of them, particularly Mrs Prentice, getting a fierce though usually inaccurate letter published in one newspaper or another. Her home is a meeting place for Palestinians and Arab nationalists of all kinds. Didn't you know?' He spoke kindly and patiently as one would explain something to a child of six. It was about what I deserved. Because I hadn't at all realised that Joanna and Robert had gone in for Middle Eastern politics. Perhaps I had missed it because I hadn't expected it of them . . . and particularly not of my Joanna. Joanna had always struck me as being one of those women who are completely absorbed by their husbands and children. She had never shown the slightest interest in politics, at least not to my knowledge.

'No, I didn't know,' I admitted. 'I'm very interested. Are you sure it is Mrs Prentice who is involved? She could of course merely be acting for her husband.'

'I don't believe so. Of course, her husband's position in the University provided a basis for it all . . . plenty of hot-headed young students around and various Arabs here on grants who would think it clever to blow in a few Israeli windows in the West End. That's the real reason we keep an eye on these groups.'

'Look,' I said, and I pulled out the photographs. 'Do you recognise either of these two? Could they be students of Prentice's?' He examined the faces, fixed for ever in their stunned distress. 'I don't know them,' he said. 'I don't know every Arab who comes to study in the United Kingdom but I would have thought from the clothes that these two were more likely to have been to Italy than here. Those aren't the clothes English students wear.'

'No, I suppose not,' I said. What would England export? Miniature Castros and Ché Guevaras? Not my men at all and yet I had hoped optimistically that this Israeli might be able to tie up all the loose ends for me.

'Spicer must have told you that my friend Duncan Stuart was very likely murdered by some nationalist group. Have you any idea who could have done it?'

'I'm sorry,' he said. 'That's not my line of country. I was surprised by your version of the affair because Mr Stuart certainly hadn't got anything to do with us. None of our people had even heard of him. We knew of his wife, of course.'

'You did?' I asked.

'Certainly. She's done some important work on Arab village life. Quite a model for anyone else wanting to do the same sort of thing.'

'Secret work?' I asked.

'Absolutely not. Academic rural economics. But it had a particular relevance to our part of the world so all our university libraries need offprints of her papers. I didn't know this myself. Someone told me when I started asking around about her husband.'

'Did you talk about it a lot?' I asked curiously. I still hadn't discovered why he had been so anxious to see me.

'Yes, we talked it over,' he admitted. 'There's no smoke without fire.'

'What were your conclusions?' I asked.

'We gradually eliminated a lot of ideas and came to this one. That Mrs Stuart had found something out . . . or drawn conclusions which the Arabs didn't like, so they went to drastic lengths to stop her talking and then destroyed all her research papers.' He paused and then asked delicately, 'I suppose you haven't got Mrs Stuart's papers?'

'No,' I said. 'I couldn't find them.'

'That's what I wondered,' he said. 'That's what we assumed.'

'You would have liked to have seen them, then? What do you think is in them?'

He shrugged. 'I don't know. It's just that if the Arabs were so desperately anxious to get hold of them, there must be something there they think would be useful to us. I'm curious, that's all. I don't suppose we shall ever know what it is.'

'If anything,' I said.

'If anything,' he agreed.

'She wasn't working for you, was she?' I asked sharply.

'No,' he said. There was no way of knowing what to believe. He could hardly have said yes. Yet I hadn't wasted my time with her diaries. There was always the possibility that the mysterious P she met so erratically when her husband was not there had been a contact to whom she handed information. If that was her line of business.

'Funny,' I said. 'I assumed that you had got hold of the missing papers. I got the impression that the Arabs hadn't got them, that they were well and truly lost.'

'I wondered about that,' he said for the second time. I could see it coming. He was going to have the nerve to ask me to look for those papers and bring them out and hand them over to him and his colleagues. I bridled at the anticipated offence.

'I'm sure you'd like to employ me now to get hold of them for you. Is that it?'

'No,' he said. 'It would be nice if they were found and published. Her own publishers could handle the job. They must know some don or other who could get them in order. No, I'm not convinced they are of any political significance. That's pure hypothesis. But it's a pity that her work should disappear when she put such skill and effort into it. Publish the papers and we'll buy all the copies we need.'

'I don't know where they are,' I said unnecessarily because he already believed me.

'No, I'm sure the Arabs have them. They would have no other motive for the murder.'

'And you believe that the same people made phoney payments to the Eytan Foundation just to make doubly sure that the Stuarts were incriminated?'

'I don't see why not. Probably someone with ambitions in oil thought that if the government were involved in a scandal over Stuart as well as his wife, they would be forced to nationalise oil production. He might hope to get your job when that happened.'

But it was Fahd, I thought, who had wanted to prevent a scandal.

'Then why did they take so much care to hush it up?' I asked.

'Whoever it was, failed, didn't he?' said the Israeli. He laughed. 'If I were you I'd watch out for him. He might try again.'

'Thanks,' I said without feeling.

He laughed. 'No, I was only joking, Mr Patterson. I'm sure everything will go well for you. Mr Spicer will do his bit and see you are not sent any incriminating documents, eh John?' Spicer nodded in his usual worried way. He had hardly said a word to me and I guessed that he was embarrassed and uneasy about the whole affair. He felt he might have gone too far. As indeed he had.

'The payments definitely all came from within England,' he said to me. 'Every single one. And over the last three years they totalled £125. Not schoolboys' pocket money.'

'No,' I agreed. Nor money lightly thrown away as a joke. I was ashamed to admit that it was more than I had contributed to any charity, however worthwhile. I had been giving bits and pieces to Oxfam ever since I left school but it could hardly amount to that much even over all these years. How mean I am.

'I value my life too much to risk my neck making a contribution to you myself, but I'd like to say thank you, Mr Spicer, really truly. You've been a great help to me.'

'Do us a favour,' said the Israeli.

'What?'

He was joking. He said, 'Persuade your friend Mrs Prentice to pipe down a little. She annoys us.'

I laughed but I knew that for some unknown reason he wanted me to tell Joanna and Robert that the Israelis knew all about them. Why, did not concern me. They probably knew what they were doing.

I didn't see any harm in what he wanted so when I got back and was sitting in the kitchen watching Joanna scrape carrots for our supper I chided her with having become a revolutionary in her old age. 'I was talking to a Jewish contact at the office this morning and he seemed quite put out by your activities,' I said.

'Oh, that,' she said carelessly. 'I haven't been mixed up in that for months now. Some people here, students of Robert's, persuaded me but it was all so sordid and they believed all their own propaganda. It's not really my sort of thing.'

'I didn't think it was,' I said with a smile. 'That's what I told him.'

We didn't talk about it any more then but there was one other thing I thought it might be interesting to know. Next morning I hung around the house and played jazz on the record player until Joanna took the children down the village shopping. Then I got the Prentices' visitors' book out of the bottom drawer of her desk and looked back over the pages. It had been kept up to date. Obviously Joanna's guests, however political, were not security-conscious. I sat down with the book and began to search backwards to see what they had been up to. There were a good many Arab names and from the vague addresses I assumed that a number of them could have been involved with Palestinian organisations of one hue or another. Fahd had come but I knew that already. What I didn't know was that Mohi el Din had been too. On three separate occasions. So much for his not remembering the Prentices, the old so-and-so. Once he seemed to have arrived with a friend but it was not a name I recognised from the Ministry of Petroleum Affairs. In fact the visitors' book didn't tell me very much. Ought it to have told me something? I remembered Joanna protesting when I had signed it at the end of my previous visit. 'No, no,' she had insisted. 'You shouldn't sign. You're not a visitor. You're one of the family. I mean it,' she had said and kissed me on the cheek. I looked through the book again to make sure and put it away again tidily where it belonged.

Later that week when the time came for me to leave, she had obviously forgotten about my special status because she pulled out the book, there was a last-minute hunt for something to write with and I was made to sign while the children looked on to make sure it was properly done.

'So Mohi el Din's been to see you, has he?' I asked, smiling.

'Yes. It was he who first got us involved with all those weird Palestinians. He made us go with him to a public meeting in London too. He doesn't like us any more now we've got uncommitted again.'

'What made you swing back again, Joanna?'

'They blew up that Swissair plane killing all the passengers . . . I just hadn't realised what desperate people they are. I was frightened. England's so safe it frightens me when people start throwing bombs. But they were great characters, you know, Mohi el Din and his friends.'

'I didn't know Mohi el Din was a nationalist.'

'I expect he isn't at home because of his job. It's just here that he can afford to be because it seems more heroic.'

We smiled. We both knew Mohi el Din and his flamboyant ways.

Chapter Thirteen

IT WAS QUITE DIFFERENT from my first arrival in El Aasima. Now I was manager, there was a reception committee waiting for me at the airport. Mohi el Din pumped my hand up and down and offered me a hundred congratulations. Fahd was there and Peter Batty, of course, and I was whisked through Customs and Immigration to the waiting cars. I was able to go straight to my house (Duncan's house) which was open and waiting for me. So I took possession straight away and buckled down to work.

I met Carole in the office corridor next morning. I had never thought to see her again, and there she was with an armful of files, my diet for the morning.

'Hello Carole, love. How are you? What's the news?'

'I'm going to be posted to Caracas. And I like the idea.'

'Oh God, Carole, what am I going to do without you?'

If I wanted to keep her I was obviously going to have to marry her quickly and make all my daydreams come true. Ask her first, ask her if she would. She was at least ten years younger than me, perhaps more. She would think of me as an unwanted has-been. I didn't dare ask her in case she found it funny. And maybe I found it funny, too. Was I really ready to commit myself to the unruffled, genuine calm of Carole's mind when what I really enjoyed were the manifold complications of women as clever as Joanna? I left the Carole problem to simmer for a little.

There was the aftermath of the Duncan affair which needed examining. 'How have things been while I've been away?' I asked. 'Any more burglaries?' I love talking to girls in corridors, the row of closed doors, the muffled sound of typing, the uncertain privacy of it all.

She shook her head and went ahead of me into my new office.

'Perfect peace,' she said.

So the other side had kept their word. It was more than I had done.

That night Batty and Pauline gave a big party for me, thus fulfilling their social obligations, and I rewarded them by packing them off on their longed-for Italian holiday. They deserved it and it was good public relations work on my own behalf. I wanted to be marked out as a man who cared. Duncan definitely hadn't.

Fahd came in a lot. He was still handling things in the desert because that was what he wanted but it was on the strict understanding that there was to be close liaison between us. If any trouble blew up in the town, I wanted Fahd in the thick of it with me.

I don't know what trouble I expected. There was none. Out on the oil field the drilling continued. Oil production rose, profitability was going up and on all sides there was undisguised satisfaction. Only the lean, golden dog running in my garden and the sight of Ali keeping his prowling watch upon company property reminded me of less happy days. Truth to tell, I had doubts about Ali. Twice he had attacked me and he might not be entirely innocent. He was a bright lad and spent much of each day teaching himself to read from a Government Adult Literacy Primer. If I had been more audacious, I should have asked him to lay aside his weapons and do a proper job of work for the company. Something held me back and it wasn't just my suspicions. Ali was a lone wolf. Ali was a warrior and it was not for me to change his identity. Nothing linked him with the government or the extreme nationalists, yet his presence made me feel as if I had a panther loose in the garden.

My new home was much too big for me but I don't like

living with empty rooms shut up and gathering dust. I had the whole house opened and cleaned and made to look welcoming. When the Prentices came to stay I would need it like that. I didn't take on Duncan's servants for he was notoriously bad at finding and keeping good servants. I started from scratch and was lucky.

I enjoyed those weeks. Carole made it a pleasure to go to the office and I had plenty of work to do there. The curse of the tropics is being under-occupied. I played tennis with Carole quite a bit now that Pauline had gone. In the evenings I was much in demand and was almost always invited out. Besides, Lady Silcox seemed to like me and many afternoons I swam in their private pool and drank china tea with her and the Ambassador afterwards on the terrace.

It was when I got back from one of these idle afternoons that I found a strange and very dirty Land-Rover parked outside my gate with an Arab driver apparently asleep in it. I thought at first that Fahd had dropped in to see me. There was a heavy-built, grizzled man, Fahd's size, sitting on my veranda. My new suffragi was hovering at his elbow, probably offering him a drink, but the visitor sat slumped in the plastic chair. It seemed so much too small for him. His baggy, dirty trousers bulged over the edge of the seat. The man was as dirty as his car. The long sleeves of his shirt were streaked all over with sand and from his weary, sunken face I guessed he was just about all in.

'All right, Issa,' I said, 'go and get the brandy,' and I gave him the key of the cupboard.

The man stood up. 'I don't drink,' he said slowly and firmly. Then he said in the same deliberately factual way, 'Your suffragi says Janet and Duncan Stuart are both dead.'

When he stood up I could see that the man had only one hand and that was damaged. He held it tucked close to him.

'You must know Fahd Mohammed Ahmed,' I said, remembering the flowers in the desert.

'I've not seen him this year.' He paused and looked me

over as though I had no right in the world to stand there offering conversation.

'Where are they then?' he asked.

'It's true,' I nodded. 'It was a tragic business. They were killed in a car crash. I'm Duncan's replacement.'

'O.K.' he said, 'O.K.' There was to be no public display of grief. Yet he was close to tears and I saw that he was right. He should have found the house filled with the movement of boys, the commotion of the Stuart family. That such a family, that such a solid woman (she moved like a tank they said), a person of such physical and intellectual substance should in one quarter of an hour be wiped from the face of the earth ought to be cause for sorrow.

I had used empty and unfeeling phrases. Tragic, I had said like a newspaper column in terms of death which did not touch me. It was his loss and it robbed him of words. His distress reproached me for all the things I had left undone.

'I won't bother you any more,' he said as if he were a liability and he turned and walked heavily along the veranda towards my gate. The chained dog yapped and strained to get at him.

Issa came back bringing the brandy and was too late. I was out of control. I didn't know who the man was but he had awakened ghosts of murder in that house. I needed to keep him and find out.

'Just a moment,' I shouted. 'If you're a friend of Duncan's, it's important. I'd like to talk to you.'

'I'm not,' he said and went on walking. His voice was disconcertingly loud.

'Of Janet's then . . . ' I tried.

'We've been driving into town since four this morning without a break. Now we're going to get some rest,' he said simply, and he climbed into the Land-Rover which drove off down the road and disappeared between the trees at the roundabout.

I didn't touch the brandy. I sat down on a chair and

thought about the man. He was a friend of Janet's, indeed such a close friend that he had come straight from the desert to see her without even going home first to wash and rest. He hadn't known she was dead. I couldn't think where he'd been hiding out for the last few months if he didn't know that.

Then I thought of someone else who disappeared for months at a time. The unknown initial P in Janet Stuart's diary took on flesh and became this eccentric man of the desert. So this was P, and when he was in the area of the wells he used to drop in at our camp. He came for fuel from our fuel dump, no doubt, or repairs at our mobile workshop. He knew Fahd and could come and go freely past the watchmen who guarded our stores. It could be that he was working in intelligence, either for the Egyptians or the Israelis, and had himself started the alarm about the Stuarts. He was certainly a suspect and yet I had doubts. I thought back to my own return from the oil field and the welcoming sight of that lanky, freckled girl who had been so pleased to see me. I knew all too well from having worked on the rigs, that when one's rest period came and one could leave for the respite of the town, the first thing one looked for was a welcome, was affection. I'd gone to Carole. He'd come to Janet, and his were no crocodile tears. He had had no part in murdering her.

I tried to behave normally, relax, pour myself a whisky and listen to Miles Davis on the record player. It rang false. I wanted to talk to that man about Janet and find out what he knew, and whether he really was P. On the spur of the moment I left my drink half finished and the day's newspapers in a jumble on the table. I'd been invited to dinner by the Consul that night and was going to be the first arrival.

I was so early that Pigeon was still tying his tie. He rushed downstairs looking damp from the shower, trying desperately to be polite and to protect me from his over-friendly and rather slobbery Sealyham.

'Now, now,' I said, 'I know I'm to blame for coming

early, but I want to ask you about something, something professional.'

He looked glum. He had learned to fear my questions.

'Someone dropped in on me uninvited today, an Englishman. And since you're the Consul I'd like to know who he is. That's all.'

'All?' he interrupted. 'Do you know how many British citizens are resident here? I don't know a fraction of them.'

'I was going to say that you couldn't mistake this one because he's been badly blown up at some stage and has an artificial hand.'

'Oh,' he said cheerfully, 'he's our local war hero, Dr Pollard.'

'I thought so,' I said, 'but who is he?'

'He works in the University. He's been here for years. You'll find him in the University Directory.'

'Do you know him?' I asked.

'No one does. With his decorations and so on he's on all our guest lists of expatriates and we invite him to things along with everyone else but he never turns up. I don't know anyone who knows him. You could try Laidler at the British Council. He'll be dining with us tonight and he's supposed to be in liaison with British teachers here.'

I knew of Laidler. I had wanted to talk to him about petroleum studies in the University but he was an extremely busy man and I had been bogged down with orders for piping which hadn't arrived. He was a poet and an intellectual with a social conscience and, since I am neither, I'd been diffident about asking him to the house. Throughout dinner he gave the impression that neither the oil business nor myself were of the least importance to him, but over the coffee when he was relaxed and talking a great deal I sat down beside him and asked about Dr Pollard.

'I don't know him because he's out of town so much,' he emphasised, 'but I know about him because it was the British Council that found him for the job here and we subsidise him.'

'Has he political views?' I asked.

'Good God, no. He's a botanist. I know nothing about botany but he has all the qualifications. Oxford, if I remember rightly. The people here think he's a good, thorough teacher. He's a bit fierce too, I imagine, but he's written some distinguished stuff on plant ecology in arid areas.'

So Dr Pollard hadn't ended up here as so many men did like the driftwood of Europe because they weren't quite good enough for anywhere back home. He was here in the desert because he really wanted to be.

Laidler accepted more cognac and said, 'Of course, I doubt whether he would repay knowing. He knows about plants in the desert but underneath one suspects he must be rather a stupid man.'

'What makes you think that?'

'These military heroes aren't likely to be clever men. It's always the obstinate idiot that gets himself blown up for his friends. The intelligent man's reaction is to run a mile.'

'I don't know,' I replied. 'I had to check a house for a bomb a couple of months ago. I could have been blown up. I did it intelligently, but . . . I could have been blown up.'

'Ah, but you weren't. It makes a difference,' said Laidler.

'Yes,' I said. That was manifestly clear.

'The British children here are afraid of him.'

'With cause?'

'I don't know. I've only met him once when his contract here came up for renewal. He's a very difficult, touchy man, and he always wants money, more money for his lab.'

I copied Dr Pollard's address out of a very old copy of the University Directory, there being no more recent edition. I hoped he hadn't moved house in the interval because I had decided to go and see him. I thought he might have some inkling where Janet's papers were. From what I had learned the night before, their friendship must have been a professional one, two academics together.

I didn't rush off to see Dr Pollard. I thought of ringing Fahd and getting a civilised introduction that way. The obstacle was that Fahd had told me to keep quiet, so he would hardly welcome this new attempt to get at the truth. Pollard was more likely to be an enthusiast for the truth but he was clearly one of these people who could not stand his fellow countrymen overseas. He had given himself to the Arabs and I didn't think he would talk to me. There was no reason why he should confide in me. He had denied quite emphatically that he had been a friend of Duncan's. It was Janet he had appreciated. He needed not me but Mrs Stuart to come booming in at his door with more startlingly new ideas about some almost defunct nomad community. He would have liked that and it occurred to me that he might like me if I was careful to come on her behalf rather than on my own.

All Janet's things had been safely shipped back to England. I had seen to that myself. So I looked round the house for part of the furnishings which he might imagine had belonged to her. I wanted to take him something that he could remember her by, to lessen the hurt. For I'd had plenty of practice with Joanna's children. When they are tearful, what they like is a sweet. They are bribable.

After several hours of inspection I decided that I must take him the birdcage. It was a white-painted Tunisian birdcage standing about four feet high. As far as I knew no bird had ever lived in it nor ever would. It was an *objet d'art*, like a miniature mosque topped with its own domes and pinnacles. So airy, so seemingly delicate, it stood on a low table in my living room as it had stood in the manager's house for years. Where it had come from I did not know. Maybe it had been a present to the company. Maybe it had belonged to some man whose wife did not like it or who had had no room for it on returning to a small London flat. Now it was presumably company property but I felt that we could spare it for Dr Pollard.

I spent the afternoon working off my aggressions, playing with Carole in a mixed doubles tournament at the club. I made up my mind that if we won I would try Pollard that night. If we lost I would take Carole out to dinner to compensate. We won and at half past seven I loaded the birdcage into the back of my new Mercedes which had now arrived. Then I drove off to find his house. As usual it was quite a hunt, for the streets in El Aasima aren't properly named nor the houses numbered. But the University has several groups of staff houses all much of a muchness and as Pollard lived in one of these, close to the students' hostels, I did in the end find it.

There was a garden with the ubiquitous eucalyptus trees, rather untended and overgrown. It looked as if all he ever did was to water it. Of a botanist I would have expected more. In fact the hose had been left running and his lawn was now well under water. His water bill was going to be quite considerable. Yet I saw why he did it. His fruit trees were laden with grapefruit, limes and mangoes. You could touch the fruit, still warm from the day's sun and promising ripeness. I squelched to the front door. From inside I could hear him typing. I didn't like to interrupt him and would have gone home like a shot had there not been the spreading water to get through. He ought to be called, if only to turn off the tap. So I rang the bell.

I was afraid of not doing things right. When he saw who it was he was going to shut the door on me. I knew it. Rapidly I put out a hand to stop him and he took a startled step backwards.

'Don't be in so much of a hurry,' he said.

'Dr Pollard,' I said. He didn't answer but stood there looking me up and down.

'It wasn't my fault they died,' I said.

'No,' he said. 'And in any case it is not for us to apportion blame.'

'I'd like you to have something of hers,' I said. 'She would like you to have it. It's in the car.'

He stood there immobile, considering.

'You ought to turn off that tap,' I said.

'Yes.' Without hurrying he went round the corner of the

house. Eventually the water stopped running. Then he came back to where I stood gazing into the back of the car.

I hoped he would like the birdcage, not think it too effeminate or too cumbrous. It was very Arab. I hoped he would see that and like it. He did.

'What a beautiful thing,' he said. 'How nice of her.' I smiled but he didn't. He had a sour, unsmiling face.

'I thought you'd recognise it,' I said.

He shook his head. 'No, I never went into that house. She came to the University. They weren't social calls. We were working together.'

'Yes, I assumed that,' I said. 'Well, do you want it?' I asked, nodding at the cage.

'Yes. I want it.'

I got it out and carried it indoors for him. It went particularly well in his house. My house and the Embassy houses, almost all the houses I visit, are European. They have complicated electric desert coolers and dappled marble floors and light Scandinavian furniture. Pollard's house was an Arab house and very dark. It was surrounded by the trees which kept out the sun. The floors were of dark polished tiles. What furniture there was shone with dark varnish. It was functional. His main room was almost totally bare. He seemed to be a man without personal possessions, no pictures, no souvenirs, nothing but piles of books and a big electric typewriter on a desk. He swept aside some books and I put the white cage down on a low coffee table where it shone whitely like a cage lantern. It looked lovely and I was pleased with myself for bringing it.

'Thank you,' he said. 'It's very nice.' He stood there taking in the transformation of his living room. Above us the fans continued to whirr. I didn't know exactly how to begin.

At last he asked, 'Would you like some lemonade? There's some in the fridge I think.' After a long time he brought it. His handicap slowed him down like a racehorse carrying too much weight. But the time it took him to get the drinks, his care, his concentration, were reassuring. They reminded me of the age-old ritual of pouring and repouring by which the Tuareg of the Sahara brew and apportion their tea. I think my grandmother took that kind of care when checking her linen. The time and the care were a token of love. He was too slow. It was that which persuaded me of his innocence.

'Why did you come to their house the other night,' I asked, 'if you didn't usually go there?'

'I found out something she badly wanted to know. Something that would have filled a gap in what she was doing. So I came straight to tell her. She'd been feeling low and depressed before I left. Particularly after having her permit withdrawn so she couldn't go and finish the research on the spot herself. I thought it would cheer her up.' We fell silent again and after a while I said, 'What a pity that she'll never know.'

'I've filled the gap in myself. I've got all the rest of the stuff here. I was working on it when you came.' He nodded towards the typewriter and a jumble of papers.

'Christ!' I exclaimed, choking on the lemonade. 'You don't mean to say you've got all her papers here in this house?'

'Yes, she left them here. We'd been working on them together trying to fill gaps and get them ready for publication. I've got plenty of room here, living alone. Why, have you been looking for them?'

'Yes. Everyone has. I was sent out from England, you know, to collect all the Stuarts' things but the papers were missing.'

'I've got them all here,' he repeated. How calm he was. How solid. Even when one is no longer a child, one goes to childish lengths to avoid things mutilated, man or beast, but, when it came to the point, Pollard reminded me of my grandmother. He was of another safer English generation.

I said urgently, 'The point is that the Arabs believe there are state secrets in those papers. Are there?'

'No,' he said.

'Nothing that would prejudice the safety of the state, say, if it fell into the hands of the Israeli government?'

'No. It's a study of local methods of cultivation, crop variations in these very primitive isolated communities.'

'And you're still working on it?'

'I've practically finished. There are only the figures for the appendix to complete now.'

I didn't fancy walking out of his house with a bundle of her typescript. There were too many students around. It wasn't safe. 'Could you bring her papers to my office when you're ready with them, then?'

He thought about it. Then he got to his feet. 'You'd better come and see for yourself . . . I don't know your name, do I?'

'It's Mark, Mark Patterson.'

'Come on, Mark, then.'

He was treating me as if I were one of his students. He made me feel about twenty years old; the age he must have been when he soldiered in the desert in Rommel's war.

He took me into a spare bedroom. There were books piled high on the floor and a filing cabinet and specimen cases and big maps pinned up on the walls. By the window was one of those big, old-fashioned, heavy leather suitcases that fasten with a strap. It even had Janet's name printed across it, J. E. Morley, as it must have been when it was new, when she first went to Roedean at the age of thirteen.

'That's hers,' he said.

I bent down and opened it, and it was crammed with papers. It was packed solid. It would weigh a ton. It would have to be taken in a car.

'Explain the problem to me,' he suggested.

On the window-sill he had stood three photographs in matching gold frames of the kind on sale at W. H. Smith: a young man and woman, very like him, presumably his son and daughter. The third must be his wife.

He saw me looking. 'My son's in Australia teaching

agriculture. My daughter's still at Oxford doing research. My wife is dead.'

'I'm sorry,' I said. Then I said, 'My wife's in America. She divorced me and went back. I have no children.' Maybe I am as bad as he is. I keep these things to myself.

'About the papers,' I said quickly. 'There are certain nationalist hotheads who would like to get hold of them. Particularly to stop them being published. The problem is to get the stuff out of the country and into the hands of her publishers. If it's as you say and there's no classified material I don't think the government itself would stop us taking it out . . . so long as no one else knows it is here.'

A group of girls went down the road on the other side of the trees on the way to the women's hostel. It was quite dark. We could hear their high laughter. We should have closed the shutters long ago. If he had thought about such things.

'Some of these points you need no longer worry about,' he said. 'For instance, the body of the book is already with the publishers. I've only got carbon copies and photostats here. One of my best students started this year at Oxford and I handed him the typescript to deliver. I never imagined there was any difficulty about it and it got there safely, because I have just received the publishers' acknowledgement and a deadline for producing the appendixes. She used to do her own indexing, I know, but this time I've asked them to see to that. I hate indexing. I can't do it.'

'What's in the suitcase then if the book's gone?' I asked disbelievingly.

'That's all her notes. The material from which she worked. She was here about five years, wasn't she? She got a hell of a lot of material together. There must be two or three more books there for the writing. In fact I've already been using some of the material with my own students and it has been used in the Geography Department too. In my opinion it ought to stay here. No one in London has got any use for it. You should present it to the University Library here.'

'Yes, it sounds as if that would be sensible.

'Would I understand it?' I asked. 'I'd like to know what she was doing.' What I really wanted was to get my own hands on those papers and to see for myself. We crouched down by the suitcase and he showed me what to look for and what to read in the graphs and figures. It must have been true what they said about him being a good teacher. Without him I would have been completely bogged down but he clarified instinctively; he had that sure gift of explaining to a layman, of enticing me into his own world of growing things and desert rainfall. We sat on the floor and I listened and read what he showed me and listened again. When I thought to look at my watch it was two o'clock in the morning and I was embarrassed. I had outstayed my welcome.

I knew he would never ask me to come again. We walked out through his living room, past the empty birdcage I was so fond of.

'I might need to look through those papers again,' I said tentatively.

'Yes,' he said, 'I am usually at home.'

Chapter Fourteen

I BEGAN TO DROP in at Pollard's house in the evenings to work at those papers. He helped me. If I asked him a straight question, I found that he always gave me a calm, considered and perfectly civil reply. For the rest he didn't see the need to talk any more than he saw the need to turn up at the buffet suppers or British cocktail parties to which he was so assiduously invited. He talked about the desert which was what concerned him. He watched the droughts with despair. He watched the camels and goats grazing the desert grasslands bare until the nomads had destroyed the vegetation on which their lives were dependent. I'd watched the camel trains bringing wood into the market and thought them merely picturesque. To him each swaying load spelled the destruction of the acacia scrub, the squandering of natural resources. Janet's trunkful of figures showed only too clearly how the oil companies were hastening the process of change. We had disturbed and replaced the local economy. We too had wasted the desert with our ignorance.

When talking over these things got us no further we played chess together in silence. For both of us it was a distraction from the more intractable problems of making a living. Confined in a small, unbearably hot town like El Aasima, one's choice of friends is not wide. I dare say we alleviated each other's claustrophobia.

Dr Pollard asked nothing of me, though in Janet's name he might have asked much. To him her statistics alone were sufficient vindication. There was nothing secret in those papers. Her conclusions were occasionally dismaying. She drew attention to the exhausted soil, the fragmentation of the land as sons inherited from father, the absentee landlords and the poor fodder resources. But figures alone did this without commentary. The problems were of the area, not of her creation. She was innocent.

Over the next few days I thought about it. I thought of getting up on my high horse and drumming it into the Police Department that the Stuarts had been framed, quite unscrupulously; that it was a scandal, that it should never have been tolerated. But then as I lay by the pool with Carole on those bright afternoons, I reflected that life had become very quiet and prosperous again, that from our point of view there was no point in ruffling calm waters. Sleeping dogs should lie. That practical, profitable English policy of doing nothing had so much to recommend it. Carole hated my friendship with Dr Pollard. We had our first arguments about it. She was with me one evening when (since it was her turn) I was going to take her out to eat kebabs at the open-air Arab restaurant by the High School. We had already been to bed. We were sleek and lazy and giggling when the telephone rang. A shrill Arab voice, a voice I did not know, said, 'Hallo, hallo. Dr Pollard is badly hurt. We do not know what to do. He said to call you.'

He sounded desperate for me to come, as if my being there would put everything right.

'How did it happen? You must send for a doctor at once.'

'Someone attacked him. Ali has already gone for the doctor.' I felt the nightmare starting up again. 'O.K. I'll come right away,' I said, and put the phone down.

'Carole,' I said, 'be a dear. There's something important you can do for me. Drive to the office and try and get Fahd or someone who knows him on the telephone. Ask him to come back as soon as he can, will you? Tell him it's urgent and I'd like him here tomorrow morning if he can make it. Ask him to fly in if there is a plane.'

I took my Boots first-aid kit out of the bathroom cupboard and went out to the car. Carole was already driving off down the road. I followed her, my wheels spinning on the dust. I don't know what I thought the urgency was. There was nothing I could do for Pollard. I am the worst person to summon to an accident. That sort of mess is for women or doctors to deal with; not me. But I drove to Pollard's house because it was clearly my fault that he'd become a target. I had to take the consequences.

The lights in his house were all on and none of the shutters closed. A group of very young students clustered at the door but at my age all students look young. They stood aside respectfully to let me pass. More boys were inside; their fresh young faces turned to me in absolute trust. Then they all started talking at once.

'Where is he?' I asked, brushing aside the confusion of Arabic. There was blood on the floor and I could not cope with their hysteria. They had not moved him. They had had that much sense and he was lying where he had fallen in the narrow space between his typing table and the bedroom door. He was unconscious and his eyes were shut. His mouth was open and blood and saliva had trickled across his face. His metal hand now stuck up like the feet of a dead insect from the polished tiles. He looked terrible. One of the students, a serious, dark-skinned boy they called Bashir, was kneeling by him.

He straightened his glasses and said, 'I think he's not badly hurt. His heart and his pulse are strong and regular, his breathing is all right and there don't seem to be any bones broken.'

'Well, that's something,' I said equally gravely. 'You must be a medical student.'

He nodded. 'Ali went to look for the Professor. He had a late class. They should be here soon. The trouble is,' he said, 'that I don't like to move him in case there's some internal injury. On the other hand, if he's only fainted, we ought to sit him up and put his head between his knees. What do you think, sir?'

'It could be concussion,' I said. I didn't know how the hell to tell, either. It could be anything, but Pollard really did look very white. The boys were waiting for me to say or do something.

'Let's wait for the doctor,' I said decisively.

We waited. They began to tell me again what had happened. This is what I pieced together. They had been going down town to one of the open-air cinemas and had arranged to meet first in a hostel courtyard just a little way up the road. While they were waiting there they heard some other boys say that friends of theirs had got safely away in a taxi and that the old English fool (tool of the Imperialists) had got what he deserved. It was a joke. They were laughing.

'Dr Pollard is our teacher,' said a thin boy. 'We began to argue with them and then we got Bashir to come with us here.'

'We found him on the floor. He kept fainting,' they said. 'Who would attack a man who could not defend himself?'

I imagined that, if he had wished to, Pollard could have defended himself quite well. Not for nothing did the British children call him Captain Hook and run away in guilt and terror. He had weight and he had strength in spite of his age. I suspected him, unfairly perhaps, of wanting to die. For I tend to think of pacifism as a kind of laziness, an unwillingness to make any effort.

I looked round at the familiar objects of his room. The bead-fringed net cover that protected his jug of drinking water, the box of drinking straws, the brown gecko high on the wall by the kitchen door gazing down round-eyed and motionless. All was undisturbed. But I could not prevent the boys from examining his few possessions, touching his books with wonder. They turned the pages and were mystified to find ochre drawings of outdated tanks and artillery. He had made a collection of early, passionate books on the Great War, by which he naturally meant that earlier war when his father had died in Flanders. He had photographs of the flat cornfield and the poplars and the cemetery by the canal that runs north from Ypres.

His own war he hardly mentioned but I think he hated it as much and that was why he shied from mixing with the British community in El Aasima. The Military Attaché, himself bedecked with medals, turned out on Remembrance Sunday with the whole congregation of the English Church to honour the fallen. He expected Pollard to do the same. But Pollard stayed at home in disgust and played chess. He had turned his back on his military honours and become a Quaker, like his wife.

I knelt on the floor beside Bashir and hoped to God that the boy was right and that Pollard had not had a heart attack. I did not want another death. So I sat and watched the gecko scuttle behind a bookcase and waited till the noise and movement around him brought Pollard round again. He groaned and stirred, opened his eyes, and said in that heavy, uncompromising voice of his, 'Bastards!'

He tried to raise himself and, with Bashir's help, succeeded.

'Who were they?' he demanded when he saw me.

One of the boys had mentioned a taxi so I searched in my wallet for the old photograph of the men who had pestered me. I thrust it in front of him and he screwed his eyes up trying to focus.

'Perhaps,' he said wearily, 'but there were three of them. Who were they?'

The students were passing round the photograph.

'Why should I know?' I asked him.

Pollard whispered, 'They mentioned Mohi el Din Saad. They said he was waiting. He's a friend of yours, too, isn't he. You've mentioned him.'

I was worried about Pollard. Except for the red bruising he was white, chalky white.

'Please don't make him talk,' Bashir said to me and I knew that, slight and young as he was, he had the situation under control. When the Professor arrived at last he also seemed too young. He spoke with a self-conscious lisp and I thought him affected but, if the boys said he was the best doctor in the University, then he probably was. He glanced down at Pollard, listened attentively to what Bashir told him, and opened his bag. Muttering unintelligible comfort to Pollard (why hadn't I done that?) he knelt and confirmed for himself. Then he threw us all out and shut the door. I must say I was not sorry. I went and got the hose and sprayed the fruit trees for him. Any activity was better than none.

After what seemed like a long time the doctor came out into the dripping garden. 'He's all right,' he said, smiling, 'though you did right to call me. I don't think any serious damage has been done. Now, all of you, off to your hostels and homes. There's no need for you here.' To me he said, 'He's very bruised and knocked about. I've put two stitches in his face to stop it scarring. There may be some internal injury which won't show up till later but I don't think so. But someone ought to stay with him tonight in case he needs more help than the servant can give. Could you do that?'

I didn't know. I knew nothing about nursing.

'Well,' said the Professor, 'I suppose I could put him into the hospital for observation. But he won't like it.'

I wasn't surprised. Arab hospitals can be a bit unnerving.

'Or I suppose you might prefer him to go to the United Clinic?'

United Clinic is shorthand for the European-style Nursing Home run by a consortium of oil companies and European embassies for the benefit of their staff. It has English nurses and an English doctor but no specialists. For specialised treatment we fly people home.

'I'd rather he were here under my eye,' said the Professor. 'I'll come and see him again in the morning. He'll be very stiff and uncomfortable by then I'm afraid.'

'What did they do to him?'

'Beat him up quite methodically and then kicked him about a bit on the floor . . . generally enjoyed themselves. I'm surprised he hasn't a broken rib for he's badly bruised.'

'And he's concussed?'

'No. He must simply have fainted. He's shocked; you might take him tea or, some brandy if you have it.'

'He doesn't drink alcohol.'

'Tea then,' said the doctor and he handed me his card with a telephone number. 'I'll give him a sedative,' he said. 'He'll sleep till morning.'

He was already asleep when I took the tea in. But he looked better now he had been washed and there was a plaster on his face. They had covered him with a sheet which rose and fell with his breathing. He was all right.

It wasn't till Abdullah, Pollard's servant, got back, and I was explaining that it occurred to me to look and see which papers were gone. There were no surprises. They had made off with the whole suitcase. As expected. I had been wondering if it would happen for I had been a regular visitor and Pollard had been openly teaching from the papers and allowing his colleagues in the Geography Department to do the same. Word would soon get around among the students. I hadn't said anything to Pollard because I hadn't wanted to alarm him. His house was often empty during the day and it would have been easy for someone to slip in and make off with any papers they wanted. It had never entered my head that anyone would come while he was at home and beat him up for good measure.

I got out one of his immense French tomes on the Ypres Salient and began to read. I thought I would read for an hour and then go to sleep in his spare room.

At a quarter past one he began to scream. I leaped out of bed, tangled in the sheet, and searched frantically for the doctor's telephone number. Pollard was screaming dreadfully and I thought he must be dying. I crashed through his house in the dark and into his bedroom where I caught my foot in the flex of his bedside lamp and brought the whole thing crashing down. Pollard woke up and at once stopped screaming. When I found the light switch and got the light on he was lying in bed blinking at me.

'I thought I was back in the Army,' he said.

'It's all right. You're not. That was a long time ago.' He was streaming with sweat. There was a circle of damp all round him on the bed. I didn't know whether I ought to change the sheets or what to do. The ceiling fans were going and I was afraid he might catch pneumonia if I left him so wet in the draught.

'I thought the doctor gave you a sedative,' I said.

'It doesn't seem much good, does it.'

'Are you in pain?'

He shook his head so I decided to leave him. I just got his flannel and wiped his face a bit. As usual he didn't seem to want to talk. All the same, those screams had shaken me.

'It's all right, Mark. It was a nightmare,' he said. 'I won't disturb you again.'

But twice again before morning Pollard woke me with his screaming. By the time Abdullah began to sweep at dawn, we were both exhausted.

'You go home,' he told me. 'I'll be all right now Abdullah's up. He always looks after me like a baby.'

I put on my shirt and tie and came into his bedroom to have coffee with him.

'How do you feel?' I asked. Abdullah had spruced him up much better than I could have done.

'Bruised,' he said. He did not complain that it was my fault. Trying to get back to sleep in the night I had dreaded him being really ill, their sending for his meek-faced daughter, my meeting her off the London plane and her blaming me, asking, 'What have you done to Daddy? Couldn't you see he's had enough?'

I did see. I saw very plainly that morning and I reacted much as the British public react to newspaper stories about old ladies who are beaten up and robbed of their pension money. My grandmother came into it somewhere and Pollard's own unacknowledged struggle to be independent. So now as I drove off early to the town I was angry, angrier than I had been before. Last night seeing Pollard lying there

I had not been so worked up. A few knocks and bruises can come from lost tempers in fair play. But that's not the same as a terrified shell-shocked man who screams like a child. I would have lashed out at anyone I met that morning . . . Arab, German, British . . . anyone on whom I could pin the blame for this injury to Pollard. There I was, driving through the town in yesterday's dirty shirt which had somehow got a smudge of dried blood on the sleeve, unshaven, bleary eyed and blisteringly angry. I knew who to blame and I knew where I was going.

Chapter Fifteen

I DROVE STRAIGHT TO the Ministry. It was early yet but I thought Mohi el Din would already be there. There's a pleasant garden in front of the building and a good strong wall to keep the mob out. At the gates is a painted sentry-box and an armed soldier in white always on guard. If you have a C.D. car or are known in the oil business, you can drive straight past him, as I did that morning, and he comes to attention and salutes like a clockwork toy.

I left the car in the forecourt.

As I went into the familiar hallway, an official, also in a white uniform, approached to be my guide but I knew exactly where I wanted to go and told him curtly that I'd find my own way upstairs. The corridors were crowded with lesser civil servants hurrying backwards and forwards with files. On benches there sat queues of Arabs waiting patiently and perhaps indefinitely to get a word with some official or other. I walked past them and went straight in on Mohi el Din.

I was right, he was there. He was sitting behind his massive, brown-painted, civil service desk behind a veritable barricade of old files. They were all bulging and all flagged for action. I wondered wherever he started. When he looked up and saw me he got up from his chair, came out from behind the desk and held out his hand to greet me. I shut the door carefully behind me. As always he was beautifully turned out but his eyes were red and there were dark smudges under them. He too had been up most of the night.

He smiled his most charming smile with a flash of white teeth and he said, 'Hallo, my old friend. So nice to see you. I thought that since your promotion you had maybe got too grand for me . . . '

If he had not been so delighted to see me, I might not have done it; if he had not been so unruffled, so satisfied with himself. I took a step backwards to steady myself and then, as hard as I could, I hit him in the stomach. I had never hit anyone in the stomach before. I had never wanted to. But this time I did it with a will and put into it all the power of my arm and shoulder. I did it because I had been cheated and because five people I cared about had now been hurt by this man who continued only to smile. I thought of him saying in the desert, 'These are my people.' I had thought he meant the villagers, but he had meant the spies, the thugs, the assassins, whom he had prevented my questioning. He would have stranded them in the desert rather than incriminate himself. So I hit him with all the certainty in the world and the effect on him was spectacular. He had been completely unprepared. He doubled up in agony struggling to get his breath.

If I had been in my right mind, I would not have done it. He could have called for help. One of the clerks would have rushed in and there would have been a scandal in which I would have lost my job. The managers of British oil companies do not go around hitting the Arab civil servants with whom they are supposed to be co-operating. But I was lucky. Mohi el Din made no noise. He staggered backwards, groping for his chair and collapsed into it. It was very satisfying. I went towards him and he thought I was going to hit him again for he cowered away from me. (As Pollard must have cowered the night before.)

'You swine,' I said. 'You could have had Mrs Stuart's papers any time you wanted. There was no need to hurt Dr Pollard.'

'I didn't,' he gasped. 'You . . . '

'No, perhaps you didn't. You're too fastidious. But you

sent some of your friends to do it. You knew how strongly they felt about Palestine. You knew what would happen . . . that they'd punish him.

'They hit him,' I said, 'just as I did you. Now you know what it feels like. Only Pollard is almost twice your age and he has war injuries. He was blown up fighting the fascists in North Africa. Did none of your brother Arabs remember to tell you that he could not defend himself?'

'I knew nothing about it,' he said stoically. I had taken all the life out of him. The fan high on the ceiling turned sporadically.

'Oh yes you do,' I insisted, 'but there's a more important matter we ought to talk about. What about the Stuarts? What about all those payments you made to the Eytan Foundation in Duncan's name, just to get him out of the way? Don't think I don't know, because I do. I know when you went to England and stayed with the Prentices and it all fits in very nicely with the times those payments were made.'

He sat up. He was on the defensive now. 'What do you mean?' he asked sharply. 'Mr Stuart contributed.'

'He didn't. The Stuarts were out here in El Aasima. Whoever made those payments made them from England where you can buy an English postal order at any post office. The Stuarts certainly didn't do it from here. But you were in England.'

'I did go to England,' he said, 'but I made no payments. You are wrong to accuse me. I knew nothing of these contributions except what I was told by our people in London and by true friends of this country.'

'Not so true perhaps,' I retorted. 'You knew Duncan and Janet. You knew what sort of people they were, that they weren't spying. But you got so carried away by your own fantasy that you let them be killed. You still won't admit that you made a mistake. A horrible mistake. You're a swine, Mohi el Din. And it's a good thing no one but me knows this little game you've been playing.'

'What makes you think I had anything to do with it?' he asked.

'Joanna told me you had nationalist aspirations, and then last night Pollard mentioned your name. Your student friends can't think too much of you, because they spoke about you quite clearly in his presence. You see, they don't count you as one of themselves. You're not a true revolutionary. You're in government service, Mohi el Din, and you can't ride two horses at once.' I was breathless and sick of the whole thing. There was nothing I could do to dislodge him or break his reserve. 'That's all I wanted to say,' I said to him.

I left his room and went down to where my shiny car was waiting. No one tried to stop me. The sentry saluted again as I slid out of the gates. On my way I passed the Under Secretary, Mohammed Ismael, arriving for work. Well, they could have a conference round the green-clothed table in his office. There would be plenty for them to talk about. How much I did not know till an hour later.

Fahd was waiting for me at the office. He had flown in at dawn. 'You wanted me,' he said. 'What's happened?'

'More trouble over the Stuarts, I'm afraid. Thank God you got here. Come into my office.' After Mohi el Din's desk mine with only two files in the In tray looked very inviting.

Fahd sat down without being invited and I said, 'It's still this stupid rumour about their being Zionists.' Fahd must always have been worried about the rumours of Duncan's Eytan contributions. He had been quick to see the harm it would do us, true or false.

'They came to get her papers . . . not the government, I think, but some student group or other and they beat up Dr Pollard who was keeping the files in his house. I think you know him. Hardly anyone else seems to.'

'I know him,' said Fahd. 'He's stayed in our camps. Plays a good game of chequers. His Arabic is much better than most of your scientists', too.'

I laughed because that was a dig at the technicians we picked to work on the drilling.

'So they beat him up, did they?' said Fahd. 'What did you do?'

'I'm afraid I went to the Ministry this morning and got my own back by hitting Mohi el Din.'

'I should have come earlier and stopped you doing that,' said Fahd resignedly. He took an old face flannel out of his pocket and wiped his forehead.

'Yes, you should. I lost my temper.' My bruised knuckles were a reminder of that.

'How is Dr Pollard?' asked Fahd.

'All right, I suppose. I keep meaning to ring the doctor and find out. What we really need to know is what they're going to do with those bloody papers now they've got them.'

'I wish I'd hit Mohi el Din,' said Fahd wistfully.

'Better not,' I told him. 'If I get kicked out you'll have to leave your well heads and pipelines and come and manage this lot.'

'I prefer to be out there.'

It was no use wasting the morning. I sent Carole for some files and showed him the latest exploration reports which had been evaluated in London. We were quite pleased with them, and were planning for the future when Carole knocked and came in again with a newspaper.

'Mr Batty thinks you should look at this straight away, Mr Patterson,' she said primly and put the newspaper down in front of me.

I could read the headline even without picking it up. It said in elaborate Arabic, 'Oil Woman's Spy Papers Found!' My heart sank. This was something we could have done without.

'Well, let's see what the damage is,' I said, trying to sound cheerful, and Fahd and I bent over the front sheet (which is the back page to anyone from Europe). There was a sustained diatribe against the Stuarts, against the company, against the British and against all Imperialists, Zionists and foreigners. Underneath, right at the foot of the page, was a small boxed paragraph saying that government sources in the Police Department and Ministry of Petroleum had issued an official denial at the highest level that any oil company employee had at any time been engaged on intelligence work or that there was anything incriminating in the papers left by the late Mrs Stuart and her husband, both of whom had died so tragically in a motor accident during the summer.

Fahd turned to me and said, 'It's a pity you hit Mohi el Din because we're going to need all the friends we've got at the Ministry.'

'Why have the press chosen to blow this one now?' I asked him. 'The Ministry wanted to keep it quiet.'

He shrugged. 'Someone young and keen and Cairo-orientated has been talking to the students or the journalists perhaps. I suppose it had to come sooner or later. What do you think we should do?'

First, get on to the editor and deny the report.

Second, ring the Ministry and lodge a protest (only they'll say they're in the clear as they've already issued a denial).

Third, ring the Police Department and demand protection of company personnel and property.

I sent Batty round to the newspaper offices. Fahd rang the Ministry because that seemed more politic and I rang the police. Everyone was very polite and apologetic and sympathetic but a fat lot of good it all did.

The Consul rang up at half past eleven. He said that they had heard there were to be demonstrations. The Embassy was going to send its people home to lunch early and tell them to stay in their houses. He said they suggested that we did the same. And they thought it best that the single girls should either stay together or go home with the married staff.

'Good luck,' said Pigeon, without enthusiasm.

'The Stuarts weren't spies,' I said.

'No, of course not. We've had an official denial from the Ministry of Foreign Affairs.'

I thought that government denials didn't do much good. One never knew who would be the government tomorrow.

I rang the people downstairs and had them put into action what I always thought of as our demonstration routine. In El Aasima a crowd gathers at the slightest pretext (the return of a hi-jacked Israeli jet, or a bombing raid over the Suez canal). We have to be prepared. We close the shutters, bar the big front door and hope for the best. Usually the police control the demonstrators and head them off towards the football ground. They don't get anywhere near our plate-glass window in the end.

The Embassy kept telephoning advice and finally Pigeon gave me his home number and said he was knocking off now. Their building would be empty. Our office had emptied too. Batty had gone back to reassure Pauline and only Fahd and I sat in the dark behind the metal doors and waited.

We both said, 'We ought to go before it's too late . . .' But what we were thinking was that we would like to stay and watch what happened. It was no good wiring London tomorrow on someone else's telex or letting them hear through Reuters that their main office in El Aasima had been burned down. They would expect more of us than that. Besides, nothing very dreadful ever happened on these occasions. The police always had the upper hand. There was no sign of any disturbance and I began to regret sending everyone home early.

Time hangs so heavy during these false alarms. I pulled up the blinds so as to get some light and tried to concentrate. If I had gone to Carole's flat, I could have had a decent lunch and a grandstand view of the square and the road towards the University. From the office I could only peer down on the street below.

The telephone rang again. Our switchboard was shut down and calls were automatically put through to my office.

Everyone was fussing and flapping. Everyone needed calming. Impatiently I lifted the phone.

'I should like to talk to Mr Patterson, please.' I heard Bill Pollard's heavy, matter-of-fact voice, and almost replaced the receiver. It was true I had implored him to let me know if he needed any help, but he could hardly have chosen a worse moment. With a crowd already gathering (from curiosity) in the square by the Embassy, the last thing I wanted was to have to go halfway across the town to help him. Surely his servant was around, or one of his students. If the man couldn't manage for himself, then he ought to be in some sort of institution for war veterans, not bothering me when I had £500,000 worth of company property to look after, no girl on the switchboard and the Police Department all apparently at lunch and unobtainable.

'Hallo,' I said. 'How are you now, Bill? Do you need the doctor?'

'I'm all right,' he said slowly. 'Don't fuss me.' It was a rebuff and I was silent. He spoke uncomfortably slowly now with two front teeth missing.

'Are you still in the office, Mark?' he said. 'I thought you might not know what's going on down here.'

'We gather there's going to be a demonstration against the company but there's still no sign of anything much this end.'

'They've set off from here,' he said.

'A lot?'

'Pretty enthusiastic, yes. And they're bound to pick up more from the cafés and suq as they go along. You know that. No, what I wanted to tell you was that Bashir has just been in with a friend to tell me to stay at home because they'd heard that the police were just going to stand aside today. They'd been talking to a policeman.'

'That's impossible,' I said.

'Have you got your police cordon yet?' asked Pollard.

'Hang on,' I said. I put down the telephone and went to the door and shouted for Fahd. Looking down from the window there wasn't a policeman in sight, not a man, not a truck.

'Pollard says the police aren't turning out today,' I said to Fahd over my shoulder.

'Mark,' said Pollard on the other end of the phone, 'I'm sure the boys are right. You must get out of that building and get home.'

'I can't go home,' I said. 'I've got to ring the Police Department. Something's got to be done. Don't you worry. But thanks for letting us know. Fahd's with me. We'll be O.K.'

It didn't seem to me that my home would be very safe either. If the police let the crowd have its way then it wouldn't just be this office and the Embassy that would be wrecked, it would be our homes. In the distance already I could hear the shouts, the rhythmical chant. So familiar, so menacing, so meaningless, 'Down Down U.S.A. Down Down U.S.A.'

We pulled the blinds again and hurried to check that the doors were locked. It was too late now.

'You shouldn't have hit Mohi el Din,' said Fahd, and he was right.

'Is the Commissioner of Police a friend of yours?' I asked. 'Could we get in touch with him at home?'

Fahd shook his head. 'No. It wouldn't help. It's my guess that the police are taking their orders from the Ministry of Petroleum. If the Ministry think the time has come to nationalise oil production then they only need some crisis like this to prove it.'

'But the Ministry can't be behind it,' I said. 'I just cannot see what they hope to gain from it. The government don't really want us to pull out. In fact they're desperate for us to expand. They haven't the capital to finance this sort of development on their own yet.'

'Yes, I think this is Mohi el Din trying to promote his own cause. Anyone else would recognise that it's the oil companies which are giving this country a chance to move forward.'

Then I said to Fahd as he sat by my desk, twisting and breaking all my paperclips, 'I'm sorry you're mixed up in this, on the wrong side. Do you want to try and leave? You might have something to gain.'

He shook his head. 'This demonstration is all nonsense. It'll blow over. When participation comes it will be won through OPEC not through student riots. Even the nationalists know that, but they get frustrated by the idea of foreign control. They need to let off steam by marching about with banners. We all listen to the Voice of Palestine on the radio and get big ideas about the Imperialists.'

I grinned at him and with a gesture of resignation he swept all the broken paperclips to the floor. Down in the square the crowd had grown and got noisier. It was chanting and shouting for a war against Israel.

> Harb, Harb, Harb,
> War, War, War,
> Battle, Battle, Battle until the liberation.

I put my fingers in my ears and went on trying to ring the Police Department. Somewhere they must have their jeeps lined up ready, but God knew where.

There was an abrupt silence, then a shout. A car had been turned over and set on fire. Black smoke rose stinking into the air.

'My God,' I groaned. I should have thought of my car. The police usually keep the students off our cars but today there were no police about. The only car left in our parking lot was my new Mercedes 250, a sitting target.

I pushed myself up against the edge of the window frame and tried to see what was happening without offering myself as a target for stones. The students in their intellectual uniform of trousers and white open-necked shirts had now been joined by groups of men in grubby jallabiyahs, the people from the town. They had found my car. I had known they would. They were rocking it violently from side to side and then with one concerted effort they turned it over and it crashed onto its roof. I thought suddenly, longingly, of the valueless things I had left in it: my bathing things, an old postcard from Brighton Pavilion which I'd carried about for years. It was just another foreign car to them and they sent it up in flames with a great cry of triumph.

The square had filled. There were students directly below us, though they couldn't see us sheltering behind the blinds. All they could see was our symbolic monolithic concrete office block which was the symbol of our hold on their future. None of them had seen how, far out in the desert, the flares burning waste gas from the oil wells light the night sky and the gigantic pipelines start over the sand for the sea. Somewhere they had found crowbars or spades on some building site and they began to hammer with them on the doors and shutters downstairs. The metal shutters are supposed to stop mobs breaking in and burning our files. The noise of metal beating relentlessly on metal became unbearable.

I knew that if the students found some explosives they would be able to break through the shutters, or even the big front door. It was only a question of time. I had thought that so long as we stayed hidden in the office we were comparatively safe because the authorities would not allow such a valuable building to be destroyed. Someone, if only the Army, would step in to stop that. Now there didn't seem to be any army, any anything between us and the flying stones.

'Come on,' said Fahd, 'we've got to get out of here while the back way's still clear.'

'What way?' I asked.

'There's a way through the gaffirs' quarters into the side alley. We'll have to run for it.'

I followed him along the dark corridors and down the back stairs. There were emergency keys in a wooden locker by the door.

'Mr Stuart once put his hand in one of these and discovered a camel spider inside,' Fahd told me with a grin. He took the key and began gingerly to open the door. The street outside was silent. A dirty child was scratching with a stick in the sand oblivious of the flies that clustered round his face. Fahd nodded and I stepped out into the sunshine and, as if at a signal, the stones began to fly at us. Roughly Fahd pulled me back into the building and set about re-bolting the door.

'What the hell was that?' I asked. There was splintered plaster from the wall whitening my sleeve.

'They can't be armed,' I said, dazed. 'That's breaking the rules.'

'I thought it was a bullet,' he said.

'It must have been a stone.'

'Shall we try it again?'

'It's too late now.' I leant wearily against the door. 'They know we're here.'

'Out Imperialists Out,' rose the angry shout from the other side of the door and one Imperialist at least would have given a lot to get out. I'd have liked to be home with Robert and Joanna sweeping autumn leaves from the lawn and fixing rockets in milk bottles ready for the children on November 5th.

The office was now being stoned from every side. We went upstairs and took our old places by my office window. At least we could see what was going on. Looking down on the screaming faces, I felt curiously detached. We get too used to watching riots on television. This one was much noisier but somehow less real. Then suddenly I lost all my certainty that we would pull through. I saw a figure I knew. I stepped out into the window to make sure and would have been hit by a stone which crashed against the glass if Fahd hadn't dragged me down.

'You fool,' he shouted. His outrage at the crowd reverberated as it turned onto me. 'Fool!' he said.

'No, I'm sure I saw Dr Pollard out there.' I said it disbelievingly. Fahd crawled over to the window. It was Pollard, there was no mistake. He was wearing a particular pair of crumpled brown trousers he had and slung round him as usual he had an old canvas school satchel. Its flap bore the faded ink initials of several children who must have used it in their turn until it passed into Pollard's more abiding ownership. He came heavily towards the square, past the burning cars and began to thread his way through the crowd.

'That's him,' said Fahd. 'They'll lynch him. They'll lynch any European they can lay their hands on.'

'He must be nuts,' I said, watching him move like an ant through the sea of white cotton.

For the second time the thought occurred to me that he was asking to die and yet his progress across the square as he was buffeted and pushed from hand to hand did seem to have a purpose, a direction to it. He had ducked the stones. He had stumbled and picked himself up again, but yet he went on and though we lost sight of him it was conceivable that he had battled on and managed to survive.

'He must be crazy,' I said again. 'Only he would think of coming out through a raging mob to fetch his students back.'

'I'm going to get him,' said Fahd making for the door.

'Oh no you don't,' I said and caught him by the sleeve. 'You're far too valuable. We can't afford to lose you, Fahd.' Though what asset Fahd would be if the students once broke through the door below, I didn't care to think. Neither of us stood a chance. We lay on the plain grey English office carpet that smelled of dust, and did nothing. Fahd began to talk about next year's expansion. He had to talk about something. He knew about numbers of trucks and men and ordering stores and piping and machine parts. It was all in his head and though I could hardly hear what he was saying above the din of the battering on the doors and the screaming crowd, I tried to listen because it was the only effort I could make.

The telephone rang then. We fell silent and looked at it. This was something we had not expected, yet still it rang until I crawled over and put up an arm to answer it. The floor by the desk was littered with stones, tins and pieces of broken bottle that had been used as missiles.

It was the Ministry of Petroleum. Mohammed Ismael sounded anxious. 'Mr Patterson?' he kept asking me. 'My dear chap, we had no idea there was anyone still in your office. Sayed Mohi el Din has just been in to tell me.'

(Sod it, I thought. They knew all right. Hadn't we been trying to contact them and getting no further than their switchboard?)

'The police will be along to you right away.'

'Then for God's sake don't let them shoot,' I begged him. If the police got over-enthusiastic and fired on the crowd it would be we who got the blame. There would be a revolution if one of those children got killed in the square. Governments had fallen for less. Besides, Pollard was out there somewhere, the idiot, and if the crowd started running I didn't know what his chances would be.

'We don't want anyone hurt,' I shouted down the telephone.

'The police know their job,' he said.

I lowered the phone and the rattle of bakelite as I fitted it back in place betrayed how my hand was shaking.

Stones were still hitting the shutters but we knew now that it was over. We could hear the police sirens in the distance as the jeeps like slow sheep dogs encircled the crowd and swept it gradually towards the south of the square. There was the popping of tear-gas canisters on the fringe. The police were slow and careful and their strategy worked. The edges of the crowd (men who wished to keep the police at a distance) began to melt away. As the clouds of gas hung in the air outside, the students beneath us began to duck and scatter, and make off for new objectives. Long after the square had emptied we could hear their chanting from the direction of the American library and hear the gas being fired at them like distant guns. But it was no longer anything to do with us.

Fahd mopped his face with the orange flannel and came

over to the desk. He lifted the phone and put it down again. There was no point in ringing anyone now. For the first time I looked at him quite carefully, at the fleshy solidity of his nose, mouth and jaw, at his expression which gave nothing away. He glanced aside and caught me looking, then he grinned. We both grinned. He seized my arm and shook it up and down and thus like champions after a long fight we celebrated our victory.

'I wonder what made them change their minds,' I said. He shook his head and shrugged. 'Didn't I tell you before, my brother? Don't ask questions. Maybe we'll never find out. Maybe they had no reason. But it's best not to ask.'

I felt that the caprice of the authorities could scarcely go that far. To turn a mob on us and then call them off at the last moment. For that was what had happened. They had called a peace between us again. The square was empty outside. The demonstration, like a piece of theatre, had left behind nothing but an empty stage littered with meaningless junk.

We went downstairs where the tear gas had already seeped into the building and opened the front doors. On the other side of the road the single line of shops was still shuttered and barred. The place was deserted. My car was a total wreck. At the best I could only salvage a few engine parts as spares.

'Let's go and get a drink,' I said to Fahd. I'd had enough. My eyes were smarting with the tear gas and we had spent too long in the office air conditioning. The heat in the square, the closeness of the air, was unbearable. By mutual consent we started across the square towards the hotel. As we went I glanced up at the British Embassy but it seemed to have survived the demonstration pretty much as usual. I later heard that it was the American library with its big windows that got burned down that afternoon.

Mohi el Din did not see fit to mention that, nor my attack on him that morning. We met him walking towards us across the square and he greeted us as if nothing had ever gone wrong.

'I was hoping to find you,' he told us. 'Mark, I have an

apology to make. I am sorry that your friend, Dr Pollard, was hurt.'

I nodded. There was a long silence and I felt myself obliged to say, 'I am sorry I hit you, too. That was wrong of me.'

'Two wrongs don't make a right,' he quoted. I knew he was quoting because the saying was uncharacteristic of him. He savoured it as if it were a profound wisdom that he had learned during the day.

He fell into step beside us and I knew he would come along and have a drink with us in the old way, as he used to do when I was much younger and neither of us was anyone in particular.

As we walked he said, 'You were right about the Stuarts too, Mark. I have read the papers now and there is no compromising information there, nothing classified as secret.'

I was just about to say I told you so when he grasped my arm and said, 'It's time we stopped dishonouring the memory of our dead friends. We must carry on with our business together. It is the oil that matters.'

I looked at him sharply, that dark, proud face.

'Yes, I agree,' I said.

He nodded. 'The Ministry, I myself, was misled by the friends of Israel. That is very clear to me now. But we should not let the Zionists succeed in spoiling our friendship.'

'Is this your personal opinion,' I asked, 'or is this the official line? Did you decide this in conference this afternoon?'

'There was no conference at the Ministry today,' he said, looking puzzled. 'I was in my office all afternoon. Dr Pollard called to see me. I told you, I apologised to him. I am sorry he was hurt.'

I was enlightened now. Pollard had done what I ought to have done to save our office. He had gone round to the Ministry and eaten humble pie. He'd saved me. He hadn't liked to involve his driver in a riot so he had had to set out on foot. He couldn't drive on Arab roads. He said he hadn't the nerve but he had had nerve enough to walk through the middle of an angry mob on my behalf and to somehow make his way past the sentry and the minor officials at the Ministry to mollify Mohi el Din.

'I had no idea Dr Pollard was coming to see you,' I said.

'He came to ask me to take a decision on the future of the papers and to beg me to return them to the University once I had had time to read them.'

Yes, I thought, that's just the sort of question a man would go out to ask in the middle of a riot. Pollard hadn't gone to bargain for the papers but to restore peace. Mohi el Din's spiel about (face-saving) friendship and co-operation was borrowed from Pollard, the incorrigible school teacher, and so too was his saying about two wrongs not making a right.

'Will you give him back his papers?' I asked, for they were his by virtue of his using them. I had thought they were mine but they were not.

'Yes, I shall send them back to him in an official car.'

'He walked through the demonstrators,' I said. 'He must have come all the way from his house by the University.'

'He's a brave man. But he came because he was worried about you. Of course no one at the Ministry had the faintest idea you were still in the building. It was a good thing that he came when he did before it was too late.'

Mohi el Din wiped his eyes to try and get rid of the tear gas. 'We had quite a talk,' he said. 'I didn't know he walked through the demonstration. He must be a brave man.'

'He has a habit of being heroic,' I said. 'He has the D.S.O. which is something the British government give to heroes.'

'Where is he now?' asked Fahd.

'He said he had to get straight back to take a class, otherwise his students would be waiting.'

'I hope you sent him in an official car too,' I said.

'It was the least I could do.'

We walked into the hotel lobby and the journalists, like

vultures, descended on me, waving that morning's fateful newspaper in front of my eyes.

'No comment!' shouted Mohi el Din and he walked grandly up to the bar and ordered the first round of drinks. We all got drunk that night and I forgot about my car being burnt. I also forgot to telex London and our head office got alarmed at the various agency reports that had been coming in. It took me most of next morning to straighten that out.

Chapter Sixteen

CAROLE LEFT TWO WEEKS later. I didn't ask her to marry me. The night after the demonstration when we were sitting together at last having that postponed plate of kebabs under the trees by the school, she said by way of conversation, 'We saw him from the flat, you know, your friend Dr Pollard. He went all the way along the street where the students were burning cars. They almost tipped one over on top of him, the people were pushing forward so. It was horrible. He was pushed and shouted at the whole way across the square and when he was right the other side in the distance near the police vans some men began to throw stones at him. They must have hit him because he started to run.'

'What happened?'

'We couldn't see. I suppose he must have got to the police cordon in time, since he's survived.' She turned her salad with her fork and then looked up at me. 'He went to the Ministry for you, didn't he?'

'Yes,' I admitted.

'You're a rotten bastard,' she said calmly. 'Letting an old geezer like that run your messages for you while you sit safe in your padlocked office. You ought to have been out there. Only you're too much of a coward.'

'If you think he's so great,' I said, 'maybe you should spend this evening with him instead of me.'

She stayed with me of course. We slept together in Duncan's big bed. Now winter was coming there was no need for air conditioning at night. I lay there listening to the indistinct night noises of crickets and cats and donkeys in the sleeping town outside. We were showered and clean and Carole lay in my arms breathing quietly. I didn't care about anything else. She was a beautiful girl. She had beautiful skin, firm, pale and smooth to the touch. I loved her cropped red head on my pillow, her careless ways. Yet the things she had said at dinner rankled. It was true I had not been to thank Bill Pollard. I hated being in anyone's debt, and I found myself undeniably indebted to him when by all reasonable standards it should have been the other way round.

I had no excuse for not going. Carole had got me back the same hired car I'd had when I first arrived in the summer. It was an unfortunate coincidence. I wasn't easy about it. It made me feel I still ought to be looking for bombs behind the mesh of the tropical seats. But Pollard's tact had laid all that to rest.

There was no need to call on him for I bumped into him next evening in the suq. He was wearing his satchel as usual and carrying one of the local woven palm baskets with its handles tied together with a bit of string. I think he found it a recreation to do the shopping for Abdullah for he was often in the suq in the evening and the traders were used to him. I was glad to see that he looked much better altogether. His face was healing.

He came round the fruit stall to meet me and together we walked along the market examining the beans and trays of nuts and clay coffee pots displayed for sale.

'It's time I thanked you for what you did the other day,' I said. 'You probably saved my life. Certainly you saved our offices.'

He looked at me and did not deny it. 'Forget it,' was all he said.

'No,' I contradicted him. 'I'll remember.'

I said, 'I'd like to see you get your teeth fixed. Go to the best man. Fly to Beirut or London and the company will pay. Can I trust you to do that?'

'Yes,' he said. 'It would be nice to get it done properly.'

I had a struggle getting the money out of our accountants, who hate anything that is not provided for in the regulations, but in the end they paid up and he flew back to his daughter in England to have some bridge work done.

'I was just going up to the lab,' he said. 'I've some experiments there which I've been neglecting. But if you like you can walk up with me.'

We walked slowly and in silence. The beggars who usually pestered Europeans in the suq hardly troubled Pollard. Perhaps his own deformity kept them at a distance. But seeing a blind child scrabbling in the dust at the side of the road, he said, 'Mark, give him a piastre for me.' I didn't take Pollard's money. I put my hand in my own pocket and threw a coin down on the sand (where the child could not tell that it had fallen, though the mother darted forward to snatch it up).

'It doesn't do any good, of course,' he said. 'What they need are the schools and hospitals that will come from the oil revenues.'

I thought then what a good man he was. It was out of his goodness towards that child and others that he had made an effort to save our oil business. His intentions were marvellous. Yet it was a sad day when goodness depended more on saving the operations of a multi-million-pound corporation than on giving small charity to the beggars in the suq.

We continued down the dusty road and onto the campus which was quiet now. Groups of students passed us on the way to their evening classes. After the bustle of the suq it was quiet and for the first time I noticed the soft stirring and cooing from within his basket. He had pigeons there he had bought for next day's lunch.

I had a sudden vision of Joanna on one of my first visits to Robert in Bahrein. She had come rushing from the kitchen in tears, dismayed at finding there the unexpected sight of three white pigeons alive beneath the table. In that heat it was normal to buy birds live for the table yet though she learned to endure the slaughter of sleepy chickens in her back yard, and even of the lamb they, like everyone else, bought to fatten for the Moslem Eid, the gentle, feathery pigeons were more than she could bear. They were so loaded with symbolism, such harmless tokens of love and peace. I didn't know that I could bear it myself; I'd eaten pigeon in the town without a qualm but I did not expect it of Pollard. It upset me that he had fallen short of some sort of moral standard I had set him.

'What's the matter?' he asked. 'I've done something to offend you. I can tell from your face.'

Then he saw me looking at the basket and he too looked down at the white birds nestling there. He understood.

'What do you want me to do?' he asked. 'Let them go free, and go without my dinner?'

I could not answer. I was soft. I put out a finger and stroked the soft, warm head of the pigeon as it trembled in his basket. All that came into my head was a line of poetry. 'Each man kills the thing he loves.' I was helpless before the immensity of the problem. There were so many things he could not do. He could help neither me nor the pigeons. He could not save them.

He went up the three steps to the lab door and then turned at the top.

'Mark, lad,' he said, 'you'll do. I could wish you weren't in oil. You people upset the equilibrium of the desert and as an ecologist that hurts me. But you'll do.' Then he shook his head and with a reproving smile set his shoulder to the lab door and disappeared inside. His students were waiting for him.

As I walked back to my car the senseless words kept running through my mind. 'Each man kills the thing he loves.' Who said it and what it meant I didn't know. Joanna could have told me. Carole was one of the things I had loved in a small way. It was a temptation to keep her, to try and salvage something from our summer together, however modest. But I had decided to let her go, like a freed bird rising to the sky. She deserved more than a life cooped up with the other company wives in the dusty confines of El Aasima.

I decided to give a farewell party for Carole. It would be a big party and I would invite everyone she knew, from the office, from the tennis club, from the American Embassy. It would be a mammoth, marvellous party just like the old days. We'd have a Lebanese mezze from the Greek caterer in town and I'd drive to the ice factory to collect ice to keep the drinks cool all evening. Everyone would stay late and those of us who survived the drinking would accompany her out to the airport in the early hours of the morning.

It was with a melancholy pride that I danced with her in my garden for hour after hour that last night. She was laughing. She seemed never to tire. Perhaps I had been foolish not to marry her but nothing could prevent her leaving now. It came as a shock to realise how glad she was to be going. Her green suitcases were already stowed in the boot of my car. She had so many of those matching, glamorous-looking cases that glamorous girls do have.

Mohi el Din, the Battys and I took her out to the airport.

'Pauline,' I said, 'you shouldn't be out at three in the morning in your condition.' But she only laughed. It was not at all a sad leave-taking.

At the check-in gates Carole whispered, 'Just you come with me, please,' so we left the others and I took her to have her baggage weighed.

She said, 'I didn't want Mohi el Din to come with us. I don't like him.'

I was surprised at her vehemence because she had been charming to him earlier in the evening. She was clearly a favourite of his since our momentous drive in the desert.

'He's all right,' I told her.

'He isn't. He's a murderer. It was Mohi el Din who murdered Duncan and his wife, wasn't it?'

'He didn't do it himself,' I said.

'He arranged it. He allowed it. That makes him a murderer,' she said in a sharp little voice. Duncan had been her boss after all. She had cared for him.

'It wasn't Mohi el Din's fault,' I said gently. 'He believed he was doing the right thing. He believed they were spying.' That was my excuse for giving him the benefit of the doubt. I had no choice. But she shrugged and said nothing. Her lips were pressed tightly together and she could have been going to cry, though whether for the dead, forgotten Duncan or whether because she and I were about to be separated by passport control, I will never know. I kissed her but there was no comforting her. She walked down the almost empty Customs hall away from me and I saw her smile her way bravely through the waiting officials. At the last gate she turned and waved. Then she was gone.

When I got back to the hall I found that the Battys had gone home. Only Mohi el Din was sitting at the little metal table waiting for me. He had ordered me one of those sweet fizzy drinks which I hate but would now have to drink because he had paid for it. Wearily I sat down.

Mohi el Din sat in silence for a bit and then he said, as if it had been worrying him, 'Dr Pollard seems to be holding it against me. I have invited him to my house, I've even invited him to the hotel and he never turns up. What can I do? I have done my best,' he added plaintively. He looked at me, expecting an answer. Yet what could I say? That our best wasn't good enough? Did he expect miracles? Things wouldn't change much, nor people. Pollard had gone on a field trip back to the desert to get away from us all, to that solace, that symbolic no man's land. We could not transform El Aasima. The poor would remain exploited and Mohi el Din and I would remain in charge, whatever our mistakes. God knows, we had made enough of those, but we were still in control and probably always would be since we were prepared to compromise ourselves and accommodate each other in order to remain so.

Mohi el Din would not have understood that. But he looked so hurt and puzzled that he had to be told something.

'It's all right,' I said to cheer him up. 'It's nothing personal. Dr Pollard doesn't go out, not to anyone's parties.'

'Never?'

'No, not even for the Ambassador.'

That seemed to convince him. He sat in silence again and we watched the people weighing in for the flight to Rome.

'You know, Mark,' said Mohi el Din who was now in a confiding mood, 'I cannot accept all the blame for what happened to the Stuarts.'

'Oh,' I said. I was surprised he had brought that up again.

'You see,' he said charmingly, 'you must share the responsibility. It was your friends who were behind it all.'

'My friends?'

'You said you still knew the Prentices.'

'Yes I do. They are very close friends indeed.'

He nodded. 'It was at the Prentices' house that we were first put onto this business. A group of people who used to come there, Arab friends. We heard it mentioned by one person and then another that these secret payments were involved, that Duncan Stuart was a Zionist, which now seems not to be true, although the payments were in fact made.'

'I'm sorry the rumour started at Joanna's house,' I said. 'That's very unpleasant.'

He nodded and ran a finger down the condensation on his glass. 'I've been thinking back over it, you know,' he continued at last. 'Wondering who did make those payments if he didn't. And though I've no proof I've come nearer and nearer to believing that she must be at the root of it. That she deliberately lied about them. Perhaps Joanna even made those false payments.' He looked up. 'I've no proof, of course.'

He didn't need proof. As soon as he said it I saw it was true. Joanna had done it. She had made no secret of it. She had said she would ruin Duncan and she had been implacable. I could see her tying up her burnished hair in a pony's tail and walking down to the village with the children and the pram to buy those dreadful postal orders that would incriminate him. They were tucked like dynamite into her handbag between her driving licence and last Saturday's Sainsbury's shopping list.

I said, and it cost me much to say it, 'I am afraid you are right.' I felt hollow. I felt nothing. I had suddenly lost all the friends I had. She wouldn't be coming out for a holiday at Christmas, now. I'd never drive to the airport to meet them all and show them what I had done to Duncan's house. I couldn't spend an empty evening writing to them about the office and Pollard's experiments and the Battys' baby. I couldn't wait for her letters any more. She was over. I knew she had murdered Duncan. And she would know that I knew.

What was it Shakespeare had said? 'Here's the smell of blood still. All the perfumes of Arabia will not sweeten this little hand.'

I got out my wallet and pulled out the smiling photograph of Joanna. I remembered that very first day when Ali had attacked me and taken it. That must have been why he let me go. He had recognised Joanna and accepted me as a friend. I was about to throw the picture in the ashtray when I changed my mind and put it away again. There was no point in being melodramatic about it. If I had to throw away everything she had given me, had done for me, I would have to throw away half of myself. She had chosen my saucepans and my sheets and my china. I haven't a clue about such things. She had given me the Elizabeth David cookery book that was in the kitchen and from which I intended to try and cook a decent meal, I who had said to her that I got tired of Arab food.

Well, we must pick up the pieces.

'Yes, she was my friend,' I said to Mohi el Din. 'I had no better friend.' There was sand on the floor and on the show-cases where they put duty-free goods on display. 'Let's agree to forget it, shall we? We all make mistakes.'

We went out to our cars and he drove away ahead of me into the night. I went more slowly, indescribably sorry. To my right the lights of the landing path glimmered. To my left lay our desert. It was the long, straight airport road where Duncan had died. I'd never liked the man and now I couldn't like Joanna who had killed him. Funny really. He had died just there. But I wasn't going to die. I was going home.

The town was quiet and dark. Houses enclosed with sleeping people. Labourers sleeping in the open air at the first building sites. The sentry at the Silcoxes' looked up as my headlights flashed past. I took the University Road. The hostels were in darkness and Pollard's house stood locked up within its neglected garden. It was late. I should have gone to bed earlier. The American Ambassador had asked me to dinner the next day. Pauline was going to give a party on Saturday for my new secretary. These were the things I should think about now. A new secretary on Monday. Duncan was dead. It was my place now.